I0660547

THE GHOST STORIES OF M. R. JAMES

10 TALES OF GHASTLINESS AND GHOSTLY GOINGS ON

Copyright © 2011 Read Books Ltd.
This book is copyright and may not be
reproduced or copied in any way without
the express permission of the publisher in writing

British Library Cataloguing-in-Publication Data
A catalogue record for this book is available from
the British Library

Contents

M. R. James

Montague Rhodes James was born in Kent, England in 1862. An intellectually gifted child, he excelled academically at both Temple Grove School and Eton College before enrolling at King's College, Cambridge. A highly respected scholar to this day, James' areas of research interest were apocryphal Biblical literature and mediaeval illuminated manuscripts. He was, by turns, Fellow, Dean, and Tutor at King's College, and in 1905 was installed as Provost. James was a highly sociable man, and he travelled widely throughout Europe.

James came to writing fiction relatively late, not publishing his first collection of short stories – *Ghost Stories of an Antiquary* (1904) – until the age of 42. Many of his tales were written as Christmas Eve entertainments and read aloud to friends. James described his introduction to ghosts in 1931: "In my childhood I chanced to see a toy Punch and Judy set, with figures cut out in cardboard. One of these was The Ghost. It was a tall figure habited in white with an unnaturally long and narrow head, also surrounded with white, and a dismal visage. Upon this my conceptions of a ghost were based, and for years it permeated my dreams." James believed that must a good story must "put the reader into the position of saying to himself: 'If I'm not careful, something of this kind may happen to me!'" He eventually published five collections of his ghost stories, all of which were reprinted and adapted numerous times.

Modern scholars now see James as having redefined the ghost story for the 20th century by abandoning many of the formal Gothic clichés of his predecessors and using more realistic contemporary settings. However, James's tales tend to reflect his own antiquarian interests, and he is seen as the founder of the 'antiquarian ghost story'. His first two collections – *Ghost Stories of an Antiquary* (1904) and *More Ghost Stories* (1911) – are generally regarded as his most important, containing as they do the well-known stories 'Number 13', 'Count Magnus', 'Oh, Whistle and I'll Come to You, My Lad' and 'Casting the Runes'.

The onset of World War One marked the beginning of the end of James' golden years in Cambridge. In 1918, he accepted the post of Provost of Eton College. He was awarded the Order of Merit in 1930, and died in 1936, aged 73.

A School Story

Two men in a smoking-room were talking of their private-school days. 'At *our* school,' said A., 'we had a ghost's foot-mark on the staircase. What was it like? Oh, very unconvincing. Just the shape of a shoe, with a square toe, if I remember right. The staircase was a stone one. I never heard any story about the thing. That seems odd, when you come to think of it. Why didn't somebody invent one, I wonder?'

'You never can tell with little boys. They have a mythology of their own. There's a subject for you, by the way – "The Folklore of Private Schools".'

'Yes; the crop is rather scanty, though. I imagine, if you were to investigate the cycle of ghost stories, for instance, which the boys at private schools tell each other, they would all turn out to be highly-compressed versions of stories out of books.'

'Nowadays the *Strand* and *Pearson's*, and so on, would be extensively drawn upon.'

'No doubt: they weren't born or thought of in *my* time. Let's see. I wonder if I can remember the staple ones that I was told. First, there was the house with a room in which a series of people insisted on passing a night; and each of them in the morning was found kneeling in a corner, and had just time to say, "I've seen it," and died.'

'Wasn't that the house in Berkeley Square?'

'I dare say it was. Then there was the man who heard a noise in the passage at night, opened his door, and saw someone crawling towards him on all fours with his eye hanging out on his cheek. There was besides, let me think – Yes! the room where a man was found dead in bed with a horseshoe mark on his forehead, and the floor under the bed was covered with marks of horseshoes also; I don't know why. Also there was the lady who, on locking her bedroom door in a strange house, heard a thin voice among the bed-curtains say, "Now we're shut in for the night." None of those had any explanation or sequel. I wonder if they go on still, those stories.'

'Oh, likely enough – with additions from the magazines, as I said. You never heard, did you, of a real ghost at a private school? I thought not; nobody has that ever I came across.'

'From the way in which you said that, I gather that *you* have.'

'I really don't know; but this is what was in my mind. It happened at my private school thirty-odd years ago, and I haven't any explanation of it.

'The school I mean was near London. It was established in a large and fairly old house – a great white building with very fine grounds about it; there were large cedars in the garden, as there are in so many of the older gardens in the Thames valley, and ancient elms in the three or four fields which we used for our games. I think probably it was quite an attractive place, but boys seldom allow that their schools possess any tolerable features.

'I came to the school in a September, soon after the year 1870; and among the boys who arrived on the same day was one whom I took to: a Highland boy, whom I will call McLeod. I needn't spend time in describing him: the main thing is that I got to know him very well.

He was not an exceptional boy in any way – not particularly good at books or games – but he suited me.

'The school was a large one: there must have been from 120 to 130 boys there as a rule, and so a considerable staff of masters was required, and there were rather frequent changes among them.

'One term – perhaps it was my third or fourth – a new master made his appearance. His name was Sampson. He was a tallish, stoutish, pale, black-bearded man. I think we liked him: he had travelled a good deal, and had stories which amused us on our school walks, so that there was some competition among us to get within earshot of him. I remember too – dear me, I have hardly thought of it since then! – that he had a charm on his watch-chain that attracted my attention one day, and he let me examine it. It was, I now suppose, a gold Byzantine coin; there was an effigy of some absurd emperor on one side; the other side had been worn practically smooth, and he had had cut on it – rather barbarously – his own initials, G.W.S., and a date, 24 July 1865. Yes, I can see it now: he told me he had picked it up in Constantinople: it was about the size of a florin, perhaps rather smaller.

'Well, the first odd thing that happened was this. Sampson was doing Latin grammar with us. One of his favourite methods - perhaps it is rather a good one - was to make us construct sentences out of our own heads to illustrate the rules he was trying to make us learn. Of course that is a thing which gives a silly boy a chance of being impertinent: there are lots of school stories in which that happens – or anyhow there might be. But Sampson was too good a disciplinarian for us to think of trying that one with him. Now, on this occasion he was telling us how to express *remembering* in Latin: and he ordered us each to make a sentence bringing the verb *memini*, "I remember". Well, most of us made up some ordinary sentence such as "I remember my father," or "He remembers his book," or something equally uninteresting: and I dare say a good many put down *memino librum meum*, and so forth: but the boy I mentioned – McLeod – was evidently thinking of something more elaborate than that. The rest of us wanted to have our sentences passed, and get on to something else, so some kicked him under the desk, and I, who was next to him, poked him and whispered to him to look sharp. But he didn't seem to attend. I looked at his paper and saw he had put down nothing at all. So I jogged him again harder than before and upbraided him sharply for keeping us all waiting. That did have some effect. He started and seemed to wake up, and then very quickly he scribbled about a couple of lines on his paper, and showed it up with the rest. As it was the last, or nearly the last, to come in, and as Sampson had a good deal to say to the boys who had written *meminiscimus patri meo* and the rest of it, it turned out that the clock struck twelve before he had got to McLeod, and McLeod had to wait afterwards to have his sentence corrected. There was nothing much going on outside when I got out, so I waited for him to come. He came very slowly when he did arrive, and I guessed there had been some sort of trouble. "Well," I said, "what did you get?" "Oh, I don't know," said McLeod, "nothing much: but I think Sampson's rather sick with me." "Why, did you show him up some rot?" "No fear," he said. "It was all right

--

as far as I could see: it was like this. *Memento* – that's right enough for remember, and it takes a genitive – *memento putei inter quatuor taxos*." "What silly rot!" I said. "What made you shove that down? What does it mean?" "That's the funny part," said McLeod. "I'm not quite sure what it does mean. All I know is, it just came into my head and I corked it down. I know what I *think* it means, because just before I wrote it down I had a sort of picture of it in my head: I believe it means 'Remember the well among the four' – what are those dark sort of trees that have red berries on them?" "Mountain ashes, I s'pose you mean." "I never heard of them," said McLeod; "no, *I'll* tell you – yews." "Well, and what did Sampson say?" "Why, he was jolly odd about it. When he read it he got up and went to the mantelpiece and stopped quite a long time without saying anything, with his back to me. And then he said, without turning round, and rather quiet, 'What do you suppose that means?' I told him what I thought; only I couldn't remember the name of the silly tree: and then he wanted to know why I put it down, and I had to say something or other. And after that he left off talking about it, and asked me how long I'd been here, and where my people lived, and things like that: and then I came away: but he wasn't looking a bit well."

'I don't remember any more that was said by either of us about this. Next day McLeod took to his bed with a chill or something of the kind, and it was a week or more before he was in school again. And as much as a month went by without anything happening that was noticeable. Whether or not Mr Sampson was really startled, as McLeod had thought, he didn't show it. I am pretty sure, of course, now, that there was something very curious in his past history, but I'm not going to pretend that we boys were sharp enough to guess any such thing.

'There was one other incident of the same kind as the last which I told you. Several times since that day we had had to make up examples in school to illustrate different rules, but there had never been any row except when we did them wrong. At last there came a day when we were going through those dismal things which people call Conditional Sentences, and we were told to make a conditional sentence, expressing a future consequence. We did it, right or wrong, and showed up our bits of paper, and Sampson began looking through them. All at once he got up, made some odd sort of noise in his throat, and rushed out by a door that was just by his desk. We sat there for a minute or two, and then – I suppose it was incorrect – but we went up, I and one or two others, to look at the papers on his desk. Of course I thought someone must have put down some nonsense or other, and Sampson had gone off to report him. All the same, I noticed that he hadn't taken any of the papers with him when he ran out. Well, the top paper on the desk was written in red ink – which no one used – and it wasn't in anyone's hand who was in the class. They all looked at it – McLeod and all – and took their dying oaths that it wasn't theirs. Then I thought of counting the bits of paper. And of this I made quite certain: that there were seventeen bits of paper on the desk, and sixteen boys in the form. Well, I bagged the extra paper, and kept it, and I believe I have it now. And now you will want to know what was written on it. It was simple enough, and harmless enough, I should have said.

' "*Si tu non veneris ad me, ego veniam ad te,*"
which means, I suppose, "If you don't come to me, I'll
come to you." '

'Could you show me the paper?' interrupted the
listener.

'Yes, I could: but there's another odd thing about it.
That same afternoon I took it out of my locker – I know
for certain it was the same bit, for I made a finger-mark
on it – and no single trace of writing of any kind was
there on it. I kept it, as I said, and since that time I have
tried various experiments to see whether sympathetic
ink had been used, but absolutely without result.

'So much for that. After about half an hour Sampson
looked in again: said he had felt very unwell, and told us
we might go. He came rather gingerly to his desk, and
gave just one look at the uppermost paper: and I
suppose he thought he must have been dreaming:
anyhow, he asked no questions.

'That day was a half-holiday, and next day Sampson
was in school again, much as usual. That night the third
and last incident in my story happened.

'We – McLeod and I – slept in a dormitory at right
angles to the main building. Sampson slept in the main
building on the first floor. There was a very bright full
moon. At an hour which I can't tell exactly, but some
time between one and two, I was woken up by somebody
shaking me. It was McLeod; and a nice state of mind he
seemed to be in. "Come," he said – "come! there's a
burglar getting in through Sampson's window." As soon
as I could speak, I said, "Well, why not call out and wake
everybody up?" "No, no," he said, "I'm not sure who

it is: don't make a row: come and look." Naturally I came and looked, and naturally there was no one there. I was cross enough, and should have called McLeod plenty of names: only – I couldn't tell why – it seemed to me that there *was* something wrong – something that made me very glad I wasn't alone to face it. We were still at the window looking out, and as soon as I could, I asked him what he had heard or seen. "I didn't *hear* anything at all," he said, "but about five minutes before I woke you, I found myself looking out of this window here, and there was a man sitting or kneeling on Sampson's window-sill, and looking in, and I thought he was beckoning." "What sort of man?" McLeod wriggled. "I don't know," he said, "but I can tell you one thing – he was beastly thin: and he looked as if he was wet all over: and," he said, looking round and whispering as if he hardly liked to hear himself, "I'm not at all sure that he was alive."

'We went on talking in whispers some time longer, and eventually crept back to bed. No one else in the room woke or stirred the whole time. I believe we did sleep a bit afterwards, but we were very cheap next day.

'And next day Mr Sampson was gone: not to be found: and I believe no trace of him has ever come to light since. In thinking it over, one of the oddest things about it all has seemed to me to be the fact that neither McLeod nor I ever mentioned what we had seen to any third person whatever. Of course no questions were asked on the subject, and if they had been, I am inclined to believe that we could not have made any answer: we seemed unable to speak about it.

'That is my story,' said the narrator. 'The only

approach to a ghost story connected with a school that I know, but still, I think, an approach to such a thing.'

The sequel to this may perhaps be reckoned highly conventional; but a sequel there is, and so it must be produced. There had been more than one listener to the story, and, in the latter part of that same year, or of the next, one such listener was staying at a country house in Ireland.

One evening his host was turning over a drawer full of odds and ends in the smoking-room. Suddenly he put his hand upon a little box. 'Now,' he said, 'you know about old things; tell me what that is.' My friend opened the little box, and found in it a thin gold chain with an object attached to it. He glanced at the object and then took off his spectacles to examine it more narrowly. 'What's the history of this?' he asked. 'Odd enough,' was the answer. 'You know the yew thicket in the shrubbery: well, a year or two back we were cleaning out the old well that used to be in the clearing here, and what do you suppose we found?'

'Is it possible that you found a body?' said the visitor, with an odd feeling of nervousness.

'We did that: but what's more, in every sense of the word, we found two.'

'Good Heavens! Two? Was there anything to show how they got there? Was this thing found with them?'

'It was. Amongst the rags of the clothes that were on one of the bodies. A bad business, whatever the story of it may have been. One body had the arms tight round the other. They must have been there thirty years or more – long enough before we came to this place. You may judge we filled the well up fast enough. Do you make anything of what's cut on that gold coin you have there?'

'I think I can,' said my friend, holding it to the light (but he read it without much difficulty); 'it seems to be G.W.S., 24 July 1865.'

An Episode of Cathedral History

THERE was once a learned gentleman who was deputed to examine and report upon the archives of the Cathedral of Southminster. The examination of these records demanded a very considerable expenditure of time: hence it became advisable for him to engage lodgings in the city: for though the Cathedral body were profuse in their offers of hospitality, Mr Lake felt that he would prefer to be master of his day. This was recognised as reasonable. The Dean eventually wrote advising Mr Lake, if he were not already suited, to communicate with Mr Worby, the principal Verger, who occupied a house convenient to the church and was prepared to take in a quiet lodger for three or four weeks. Such an arrangement was precisely what Mr Lake desired. Terms were easily agreed upon, and early in December, like another Mr Datchery (as he remarked to himself), the investigator found himself in the occupation of a very comfortable room in an ancient and 'cathedraly' house.

One so familiar with the customs of Cathedral churches, and treated with such obvious consideration by the Dean and Chapter of this Cathedral in particular, could not fail to command the respect of the Head Verger. Mr Worby even acquiesced in certain modifications of statements he had been accustomed to offer for years to parties of visitors. Mr Lake, on his part, found the Verger a very cheery companion, and took advantage of any occasion that presented itself for enjoying his conversation when the day's work was over.

One evening, about nine o'clock, Mr Worby knocked at his lodger's door. 'I've occasion,' he said, 'to go across to the Cathedral, Mr Lake, and I think I made you a promise when I did so next I would give you the opportunity to see what it looked like at night time. It's quite fine and dry outside, if you care to come.'

'To be sure I will; very much obliged to you, Mr Worby, for thinking of it, but let me get my coat.'

'Here it is, sir, and I've another lantern here that you'll find advisable for the steps, as there's no moon.'

'Anyone might think we were Jasper and Durdles, over again, mightn't they?' said Lake, as they crossed the close, for he had ascertained that the Verger had read *Edwin Drood*.

'Well, so they might,' said Mr Worby, with a short laugh, 'though I don't know whether we ought to take it as a compliment. Odd ways, I often think, they had at that Cathedral, don't it seem so to you, sir? Full choral matins at seven o'clock in the morning all the year round. Wouldn't suit our boys' voices nowadays, and I think there's one or two of the men would be applying for a rise if the Chapter was to bring it in – particular the alltoes.'

They were now at the south-west door. As Mr Worby was unlocking it, Lake said, 'Did you ever find anybody locked in here by accident?'

'Twice I did. One was a drunk sailor; however he got in I

don't know. I s'pose he went to sleep in the service, but by the time I got to him he was praying fit to bring the roof in. Lor'! what a noise that man did make! said it was the first time he'd been inside a church for ten years, and blest if ever he'd try it again. The other was an old sheep: them boys it was, up to their games. That was the last time they tried it on, though. There, sir, now you see what we look like; our late Dean used now and again to bring parties in, but he preferred a moonlight night, and there was a piece of verse he'd say to 'em, relating to a Scotch cathedral, I understand; but I don't know; I almost think the effect's better when it's all dark-like. Seems to add to the size and height. Now if you won't mind stopping somewhere in the nave while I go up into the choir where my business lays, you'll see what I mean.'

Accordingly Lake waited, leaning against a pillar, and watched the light wavering along the length of the church, and up the steps into the choir, until it was intercepted by some screen or other furniture, which only allowed the reflection to be seen on the piers and roof. Not many minutes had passed before Worby reappeared at the door of the choir and by waving his lantern signalled to Lake to rejoin him.

'I suppose it *is* Worby, and not a substitute,' thought Lake to himself, as he walked up the nave. There was, in fact, nothing untoward. Worby showed him the papers which he had come to fetch out of the Dean's stall, and asked him what he thought of the spectacle: Lake agreed that it was well worth seeing. 'I suppose,' he said, as they walked towards the altar-steps together, 'that you're too much used to going about here at night to feel nervous – but you must get a start every now and then, don't you, when a book falls down or a door swings to?'

'No, Mr Lake, I can't say I think much about noises, not nowadays: I'm much more afraid of finding an escape of gas or a burst in the stove pipes than anything else. Still there have been times, years ago. Did you notice that plain altar-tomb there – fifteenth century we say it is, I don't know if you agree to that? Well, if you didn't look at it, just come back and give it a glance, if you'd be so good.' It was on the north side of the choir, and rather awkwardly placed: only about three feet from the enclosing stone screen. Quite plain, as the Verger had said, but for some ordinary stone panelling. A metal cross of some size on the northern side (that next to the screen) was the solitary feature of any interest.

Lake agreed that it was not earlier than the Perpendicular period: 'But,' he said, 'unless it's the tomb of some remarkable person, you'll forgive me for saying that I don't think it's particularly noteworthy.'

'Well, I can't say as it is the tomb of anybody noted in 'istory,' said Worby, who had a dry smile on his face, 'for we don't own any record whatsoever of who it was put up to. For all that, if you've half an hour to spare, sir, when we get back to the house, Mr Lake, I could tell you a tale about that tomb. I won't begin on it now; it strikes cold here, and we don't want to be dawdling about all night.'

'Of course I should like to hear it immensely.'

'Very well, sir, you shall. Now if I might put a question to you,' he went on, as they passed down the choir aisle, 'in our little local guide – and not only there, but in the little book on our Cathedral in the series – you'll find it stated that this portion of the building was erected previous to the twelfth century. Now of course I should be glad enough to take that view, but – mind the step, sir – but, I put it to you – does the lay of the stone 'ere in this portion of the wall' (which he tapped with his key), 'does it to your eye carry the flavour of what you might call Saxon masonry? No, I thought not; no more it does to me: now, if you'll believe me, I've said as much to those men – one's the librarian of our Free Library here, and the other came down from London on purpose – fifty times, if I have once, but I might just as well have talked to that bit of stonework. But there it is, I suppose everyone's got their opinions.'

The discussion of this peculiar trait of human nature occupied Mr Worby almost up to the moment when he and Lake re-entered the former's house. The condition of the fire in Lake's sitting-room led to a suggestion from Mr Worby that they should finish the evening in his own parlour. We find them accordingly settled there some short time afterwards.

Mr Worby made his story a long one, and I will not undertake to tell it wholly in his own words, or in his own order. Lake committed the substance of it to paper immediately after hearing it, together with some few passages of the narrative which had fixed themselves *verbatim* in his mind; I shall probably find it expedient to condense Lake's record to some extent.

Mr Worby was born, it appeared, about the year 1828. His father before him had been connected with the Cathedral, and likewise his grandfather. One or both had been choristers, and in later life both had done work as mason and carpenter respectively about the fabric. Worby himself, though possessed, as he frankly acknowledged, of an indifferent voice, had been drafted into the choir at about ten years of age.

It was in 1840 that the wave of the Gothic revival smote the Cathedral of Southminster. 'There was a lot of lovely stuff went then, sir,' said Worby, with a sigh. 'My father couldn't hardly believe it when he got his orders to clear out the choir. There was a new dean just come in – Dean Burscough it was – and my father had been 'prenticed to a good firm of joiners in the city, and knew what good work was when he saw it. Crool it was, he used to say: all that beautiful wainscot oak, as good as the day it was put up, and garlands-like of foliage and fruit, and lovely old gilding work on the coats of arms and the organ pipes. All went to the timber yard – every bit except some little pieces worked up in the Lady Chapel, and 'ere in this overmantel. Well – I may be mistook, but I say our choir never looked as well since. Still there was a lot found out about the history of the church, and no doubt but what it did stand in need of repair. There was very few winters passed but what we'd lose a pinnicle.' Mr Lake expressed his concurrence with Worby's views of restoration, but owns to a fear about this point lest the story proper should never be reached. Possibly this was perceptible in his manner.

Worby hastened to reassure him, 'Not but what I could carry on about that topic for hours at a time, and do so when I see my opportunity. But Dean Burscough he was very set on the Gothic period, and nothing would serve him but everything must be made agreeable to that. And one morning after service he appointed for my father to meet him in the choir, and he came back after he'd taken off his robes in the vestry, and he'd got a roll of paper with him, and the verger that was then brought in a table, and they begun spreading it out on the table with prayer books to keep it down, and my father helped 'em, and he saw it was a picture of the inside of a choir in a Cathedral; and the Dean – he was a quick-spoken gentleman – he says, "Well, Worby, what do you think of that?" "Why," says my father, "I don't think I 'ave the pleasure of knowing that view. Would that be Hereford Cathedral, Mr Dean?" "No, Worby," says the Dean, "that's Southminster Cathedral as we hope to see it before many years." "Indeed, sir," says my father, and that was all he did say – leastways to the Dean – but he used to tell me he felt really faint in himself when he looked round our choir as I can remember it, all comfortable and furnished-like, and then see this nasty little dry picter, as he called it, drawn out by some London architect. Well, there I am again. But you'll see what I mean if you look at this old view.'

Worby reached down a framed print from the wall. 'Well, the long and the short of it was that the Dean he handed over to my father a copy of an order of the Chapter that he was to clear out every bit of the choir – make a clean sweep – ready for the new work that was being designed up in town, and he was to put it in hand as soon as ever he could get the breakers together. Now then, sir, if you look at that view, you'll see where the pulpit used to stand: that's what I want you to notice, if you please.' It was, indeed, easily seen; an unusually large structure of timber with a domed sounding-board, standing at the east end of the stalls on the north side of the choir, facing the bishop's throne. Worby proceeded to explain that during the alterations, services were held in the nave, the members of the choir being thereby disappointed of an anticipated holiday, and the organist in particular incurring the suspicion of having wilfully damaged the mechanism of the temporary organ that was hired at considerable expense from London.

The work of demolition began with the choir screens and organ loft, and proceeded gradually eastwards, disclosing, as Worby said, many interesting features of older work. While this was going on, the members of the Chapter were, naturally, in and about the choir a great deal, and it soon became apparent to the elder Worby – who could not help overhearing some of their talk – that, on the part of the senior Canons especially, there must have been a good deal of disagreement before the policy now being carried out had been adopted. Some were of opinion that they should catch their deaths of cold in the return-stalls, unprotected by a screen from the draughts in the nave: others objected to being exposed to the view of persons in the choir aisles, especially, they said, during the sermons, when they found it helpful to listen in a posture which was liable to misconstruction. The strongest opposition, however, came from the oldest of the body, who up to the last moment objected to the removal of the pulpit. 'You ought not to touch it, Mr Dean,' he said with great emphasis one morning, when the two were standing before it: 'you don't know what mischief you may do.' 'Mischief? it's not a work of any particular merit, Canon.' 'Don't call me Canon,' said the old man with great asperity, 'that is, for thirty years I've been known as Dr Ayloff, and I shall be obliged, Mr Dean, if you would kindly humour me in that matter. And as to the pulpit (which I've preached from for thirty years, though I don't insist on that), all I'll say is, I *know* you're doing wrong in moving it.' 'But what sense could there be, my dear Doctor, in leaving it where it is, when we're fitting up the rest of the choir in a totally different *style*? What reason could be given – apart from the look of the thing?' 'Reason! reason!' said old Dr Ayloff; 'if you young men – if I may say so without any disrespect, Mr Dean – if you'd only listen to reason a little, and not be always asking for it, we should get on better. But there, I've said my say.' The old gentleman hobbled off, and as it proved, never entered the Cathedral again. The season – it was a hot summer – turned sickly on a sudden. Dr Ayloff was one of the first to go, with some affection of the muscles of the thorax, which took him painfully at night. And at many services the number of choirmen and boys was very thin.

Meanwhile the pulpit had been done away with. In fact, the sounding-board (part of which still exists as a table in a summerhouse in the palace garden) was taken down within an hour or two of Dr Ayloff's protest. The removal of the base – not effected without considerable trouble – disclosed to view, greatly to the exultation of the restoring party, an altar-tomb – the tomb, of course, to which Worby had attracted Lake's attention that same evening. Much fruitless research was expended in attempts to identify the occupant; from that day to this he has never had a name put to him. The structure had been most carefully boxed in under the pulpit-base, so that such slight ornament as it possessed was not defaced; only on the north side of it there was what looked like an injury; a gap between two of the slabs composing the side. It might be two or three inches across. Palmer, the mason, was directed to fill it up in a week's time, when he came to do some other small jobs near that part of the choir.

The season was undoubtedly a very trying one. Whether the church was built on a site that had once been a marsh, as was suggested, or for whatever reason, the residents in its immediate neighbourhood had, many of them, but little enjoyment of the exquisite sunny days and the calm nights of August and September. To several of the older people – Dr Ayloff, among others, as we have seen – the summer proved downright fatal, but even among the younger, few escaped either a sojourn in bed for a matter of weeks, or at the least, a brooding sense of oppression, accompanied by hateful nightmares. Gradually there formulated itself a suspicion – which grew into a conviction – that the alterations in the Cathedral had something to say in the matter. The widow of a former old verger, a pensioner of the Chapter of Southminster, was visited by dreams, which she retailed to her friends, of a shape that slipped out of the little door of the south transept as the dark fell in, and flitted – taking a fresh direction every night – about the Close, disappearing for a while in house after house, and finally emerging again when the night sky was paling. She could see nothing of it, she said, but that it was a moving form: only she had an impression that when it returned to the church, as it seemed to do in the end of the dream, it turned its head: and then, she could not tell why, but she thought it had red eyes. Worby remembered hearing the old lady tell this dream at a tea-party in the house of the chapter clerk. Its recurrence might, perhaps, he said, be taken as a symptom of approaching illness; at any rate before the end of September the old lady was in her grave.

The interest excited by the restoration of this great church was not confined to its own county. One day that summer an F.S.A., of some celebrity, visited the place. His business was to write an account of the discoveries that had been made, for the Society of Antiquaries, and his wife, who accompanied him, was to make a series of illustrative drawings for his report. In the morning she employed herself in making a general sketch of the choir; in the afternoon she devoted herself to details. She first drew the newly-exposed altar-tomb, and when that was finished, she called her husband's attention to a beautiful piece of diaper-ornament on the screen just behind it, which had, like the tomb itself, been completely concealed by the pulpit. Of course, he said, an illustration of that must be made; so she seated herself on the tomb and began a careful drawing which occupied her till dusk.

Her husband had by this time finished his work of measuring and description, and they agreed that it was time to be getting back to their hotel. 'You may as well brush my skirt, Frank,' said the lady, 'it must have got covered with dust, I'm sure.' He obeyed dutifully; but, after a moment, he said, 'I don't know whether you value this dress particularly, my dear, but I'm inclined to think it's seen its best days. There's a great bit of it gone.' 'Gone? Where?' said she. 'I don't know where it's gone, but it's off at the bottom edge behind here.' She pulled it hastily into sight, and was horrified to find a jagged tear extending some way into the substance of the stuff; very much, she said, as if a dog had rent it away. The dress was, in any case, hopelessly spoilt, to her great vexation, and though they looked everywhere, the missing piece could not be found. There were many ways, they concluded, in which the injury might have come about, for the choir was full of old bits of woodwork with nails sticking out of them. Finally, they could only suppose that one of these had caused the mischief, and that the workmen, who had been about all day, had carried off that particular piece with the fragment of dress still attached to it.

It was about this time, Worby thought, that his little dog began to wear an anxious expression when the hour for it to be put into the shed in the back yard approached. (For his mother had ordained that it must not sleep in the house.) One evening, he said, when he was just going to pick it up and carry it out, it looked at him 'like a Christian, and waved its 'and, and, I was going to say – well, you know 'ow they do carry on sometimes, and the end of it was I put it under my coat, and 'uddled it upstairs – and I'm afraid I as good as deceived my poor mother on the subject. After that the dog acted very artful with 'iding itself under the bed for half an hour or more before bedtime came, and we worked it so as my mother never found out what we'd done.' Of course Worby was glad of its company anyhow, but more particularly when the nuisance that is still remembered in Southminster as 'the crying' set in.

'Night after night,' said Worby, 'that dog seemed to know it was coming; he'd creep out, he would, and snuggle into the bed and cuddle right up to me shivering, and when the crying come he'd be like a wild thing, shoving his head under my arm, and I was fully near as bad. Six or seven times we'd hear it, not more, and when he'd dror out his 'ed again I'd know it was over for that night. What was it like, sir? Well, I never heard but one thing that seemed to hit it off. I happened to be playing about in the Close, and there was two of the Canons met and said "Good morning" one to another. "Sleep well last night?" says one – it was Mr Henslow that one, and Mr Lyall was the other. "Can't say I did," says Mr Lyall, "rather too much of Isaiah xxxiv. 14 for me." "xxxiv. 14," says Mr Henslow, "what's that?" "You call yourself a Bible reader!" says Mr Lyall. (Mr Henslow, you must know, he was one of what used to be termed Simeon's lot – pretty much what we should call the Evangelical party.) "You go and look it up." I wanted to know what he was getting at myself, and so off I ran home and got out my own Bible, and there it was: "the satyr shall cry to his fellow." Well, I thought, is that what we've been listening to these past nights? and I tell you it made me look over my shoulder a time or two. Of course I'd asked my father and mother about what it could be before that, but they both said it was most likely cats: but they spoke very short, and I could see they was troubled. My word! that was a noise – 'ungry-like, as if it was calling after someone that wouldn't come. If ever you felt you wanted company, it would be when you was waiting for it to begin again. I believe two or three nights there was men put on to watch in different parts of the Close; but they all used to get together in one corner, the nearest they could to the High Street, and nothing came of it.

'Well, the next thing was this. Me and another of the boys – he's in business in the city now as a grocer, like his father before him – we'd gone up in the choir after morning service was over, and we heard old Palmer the mason bellowing to some of his men. So we went up nearer, because we knew he was a rusty old chap and there might be some fun going. It appears Palmer 'd told this man to stop up the chink in that old tomb. Well, there was this man keeping on saying he'd done it the best he could, and there was Palmer carrying on like all possessed about it. "Call that making a job of it?" he says. "If you had your rights you'd get the sack for this. What do you suppose I pay you your wages for? What do you suppose I'm going to say to the Dean and Chapter when they come round, as come they may do any time, and see where you've been bungling about covering the 'ole place with mess and plaster and Lord knows what?" "Well, master, I done the best I could," says the man; "I don't know no more than what you do 'ow it come to fall out this way. I tamped it right in the 'ole," he says, "and now it's fell out," he says, "I never see."

' "Fell out?" says old Palmer, "why it's nowhere near the place. Blowed out, you mean"; and he picked up a bit of plaster, and so did I, that was laying up against the screen, three or four feet off, and not dry yet; and old Palmer he looked at it curious-like, and then he turned round on me and he says, "Now then, you boys, have you been up to some of your games here?"

"No," I says, "I haven't, Mr Palmer; there's none of us been about here till just this minute"; and while I was talking the other boy, Evans, he got looking in through the chink, and I heard him draw in his breath, and he came away sharp and up to us, and says he, "I believe there's something in there. I saw something shiny." "What! I dare say!" says old Palmer; "well, I ain't got time to stop about there. You, William, you go off and get some more stuff and make a job of it this time; if not, there'll be trouble in my yard," he says.

'So the man he went off, and Palmer too, and us boys stopped behind, and I says to Evans, "Did you really see anything in there?" "Yes," he says, "I did indeed." So then I says, "Let's shove something in and stir it up." And we tried several of the bits of wood that was laying about, but they were all too big. Then Evans he had a sheet of music he'd brought with him, an anthem or a service, I forget which it is now, and he rolled it up small and shoved it in the chink; two or three times he did it, and nothing happened. "Give it me, boy," I said, and I had a try. No, nothing happened. Then, I don't know why I thought of it, I'm sure, but I stooped down just opposite the chink and put my two fingers in my mouth and whistled – you know the way – and at that I seemed to think I heard something stirring, and I says to Evans, "Come away," I says; "I don't like this," "Oh, rot," he says, "give me that roll," and he took it and shoved it in. And I don't think ever I see anyone go so pale as he did. "I say, Worby," he says, "it's caught, or else someone's got hold of it." "Pull it out or leave it," I says. "Come and let's get off." So he gave a good pull, and it came away. Leastways most of it did, but the end was gone. Torn off it was, and Evans looked at it for a second and then he gave a sort of a croak and let it drop, and we both made off out of there as quick as ever we could. When we got outside Evans says to me, "Did you see the end of that paper?" "No," I says, "only it was torn." "Yes, it was," he says, "but it was wet too, and black!" Well, partly because of the fright we had, and partly because that music was wanted in a day or two, and we knew there'd be a set-out about it with the organist, we didn't say nothing to anyone else, and I suppose the workmen they swept up the bit that was left along with the rest of the rubbish. But Evans, if you were to ask him this very day about it, he'd stick to it he saw that paper wet and black at the end where it was torn.'

After that the boys gave the choir a wide berth, so that Worby was not sure what was the result of the mason's renewed mending of the tomb. Only he made out from fragments of conversation dropped by the workmen passing through the choir that some difficulty had been met with, and that the governor – Mr Palmer to wit – had tried his own hand at the job. A little later, he happened to see Mr Palmer himself knocking at the door of the Deanery and being admitted by the butler. A day or so after that, he gathered from a remark his father let fall at breakfast, that something a little out of the common was to be done in the Cathedral after morning service on the morrow. 'And I'd just as soon it was today,' his father added; 'I don't see the use of running risks.' ' "Father," I says, "what are you going to do in the Cathedral tomorrow?" And he turned on me as savage as I ever see him – he was a wonderful good-tempered man as a general thing, my poor father was. "My lad," he says, "I'll trouble you not to go picking up your elders' and betters' talk: it's not manners and it's not straight. What I'm going to do or not going to do in the Cathedral tomorrow is none of your business: and if I catch sight of you hanging about the place tomorrow after your work's done, I'll send you home with a flea in your ear. Now you mind that." Of course I said I was very sorry and that, and equally of course I went off and laid my plans with Evans. We knew there was a stair up in the corner of the transept which you can get up to the triforium, and in them days the door to it was pretty well always open, and even if it wasn't we knew the key usually laid under a bit of matting hard by. So we made up our minds we'd be putting away music and that, next morning while the rest of the boys was clearing off, and then slip up the stairs and watch from the triforium if there was any signs of work going on.

'Well, that same night I dropped off asleep as sound as a boy does, and all of a sudden the dog woke me up, coming into the bed, and thought I, now we're going to get it sharp, for he seemed more frightened than usual. After about five minutes sure enough came this cry. I can't give you no idea what it was like; and so near too – nearer than I'd heard it yet – and a funny thing, Mr Lake, you know what a place this Close is for an echo, and particular if you stand this side of it. Well, this crying never made no sign of an echo at all. But, as I said, it was dreadful near this night; and on the top of the start I got with hearing it, I got another fright; for I heard something rustling outside in the passage. Now to be sure I thought I was done; but I noticed the dog seemed to perk up a bit, and next there was someone whispered outside the door, and I very near laughed out loud, for I knew it was my father and mother that had got out of bed with the noise. "Whatever is it?" says my mother. "Hush! I don't know," says my father, excited-like, "don't disturb the boy. I hope he didn't hear nothing."

'So, me knowing they were just outside, it made me bolder, and I slipped out of bed across to my little window – giving on the Close – but the dog he bored right down to the bottom of the bed – and I looked out. First go off I couldn't see anything. Then right down in the shadow under a buttress I made out what I shall always say was two spots of red – a dull red it was – nothing like a lamp or a fire, but just so as you could pick 'em out of the black shadow. I hadn't but just sighted 'em when it seemed we wasn't the only people that had been disturbed, because I see a window in a house on the left-hand side become lighted up, and the light moving. I just turned my head to make sure of it, and then looked back into the shadow for those two red things, and they were gone, and for all I peered about and stared, there was not a sign more of them. Then come my last fright that night – something come against my bare leg – but that was all right: that was my little dog had come out of bed, and prancing about making a great to-do, only holding his tongue, and me seeing he was quite in spirits again, I took him back to bed and we slept the night out!

'Next morning I made out to tell my mother I'd had the dog in my room, and I was surprised, after all she'd said about it before, how quiet she took it. "Did you?" she says. "Well, by good rights you ought to go without your breakfast for doing such a thing behind my back: but I don't know as there's any great harm done, only another time you ask my permission, do you hear?" A bit after that I said something to my father about having heard cats again "*Cats* " he says; and he looked over at my poor mother, and she coughed and he says, "Oh! ah! yes, cats. I believe I heard 'em myself."

'That was a funny morning altogether: nothing seemed to go right. The organist he stopped in bed, and the minor Canon he forgot it was the 19th day and waited for the *Venite*; and after a bit the deputy he set off playing the chant for evensong, which was a minor; and then the Decani boys were laughing so much they couldn't sing, and when it came to the anthem the solo boy he got took with the giggles, and made out his nose was bleeding, and shoved the book at me what hadn't practised the verse and wasn't much of a singer if I had known it. Well, things was rougher, you see, fifty years ago, and I got a nip from the counter-tenor behind me that I remembered.

'So we got through somehow, and neither the men nor the boys weren't by way of waiting to see whether the Canon in residence – Mr Henslow it was – would come to the vestries and fine 'em, but I don't believe he did: for one thing I fancy he'd read the wrong lesson for the first time in his life, and knew it. Anyhow, Evans and me didn't find no difficulty in slipping up the stairs as I told you, and when we got up we laid ourselves down flat on our stomachs where we could just stretch our heads out over the old tomb, and we hadn't but just done so when we heard the verger that was then, first shutting the iron porch-gates and locking the south-west door, and then the transept door, so we knew there was something up, and they meant to keep the public out for a bit.

'Next thing was, the Dean and the Canon come in by their door on the north, and then I see my father, and old Palmer, and a couple of their best men, and Palmer stood a talking for a bit with the Dean in the middle of the choir. He had a coil of rope and the men had crows. All of 'em looked a bit nervous. So there they stood talking, and at last I heard the Dean say, "Well, I've no time to waste, Palmer. If you think this'll satisfy Southminster people, I'll permit it to be done; but I must say this, that never in the whole course of my life have I heard such arrant nonsense from a practical man as I have from you. Don't you agree with me, Henslow?" As far as I could hear Mr Henslow said something like "Oh welll we're told, aren't we, Mr Dean, not to judge others?" And the Dean he gave a kind of sniff, and walked straight up to the tomb, and took his stand behind it with his back to the screen, and the others they come edging up rather gingerly. Henslow, he stopped on the south side and scratched on his chin, he did. Then the Dean spoke up: "Palmer," he says, "which can you do easiest, get the slab off the top, or shift one of the side slabs?"

'Old Palmer and his men they pottered about a bit looking round the edge of the top slab and sounding the sides on the south and east and west and everywhere but the north. Henslow said something about it being better to have a try at the south side, because there was more light and more room to move about in. Then my father, who'd been 'awatching of them, went round to the north side, and knelt down and felt the slab by the

chink, and he got up and dusted his knees and says to the Dean:
"Beg pardon, Mr Dean, but I think if Mr Palmer'll try this here
slab he'll find it'll come out easy enough. Seems to me one of
the men could prise it out with his crow by means of this
chink." "Ah! thank you, Worby," says the Dean; "that's a good
suggestion. Palmer, let one of your men do that, will you?"

'So the man come round, and put his bar in and bore on it,
and just that minute when they were all bending over, and we
boys got our heads well over the edge of the triforium, there
came a most fearful crash down at the west end of the choir, as
if a whole stack of big timber had fallen down a flight of stairs.
Well, you can't expect me to tell you everything that happened
all in a minute. Of course there was a terrible commotion. I
heard the slab fall out, and the crowbar on the floor, and I
heard the Dean say, "Good God!"

'When I looked down again I saw the Dean tumbled over on
the floor, the men was making off down the choir, Henslow was
just going to help the Dean up, Palmer was going to stop the
men (as he said afterwards) and my father was sitting on the
altar step with his face in his hands. The Dean he was very
cross. "I wish to goodness you'd look where you're coming to,
Henslow," he says. "Why you should all take to your heels
when a stick of wood tumbles down I cannot imagine"; and all
Henslow could do, explaining he was right away on the other
side of the tomb, would not satisfy him.

'Then Palmer came back and reported there was nothing to
account for this noise and nothing seemingly fallen down, and
when the Dean finished feeling of himself they gathered round
– except my father, he sat where he was – and someone
lighted up a bit of candle and they looked into the tomb.
"Nothing there," says the Dean, "what did I tell you? Stay!
here's something. What's this? a bit of music paper, and a piece
of torn stuff – part of a dress it looks like. Both quite modern –
no interest whatever. Another time perhaps you'll take the advice

of an educated man" – or something like that, and off he went, limping a bit, and out through the north door, only as he went he called back angry to Palmer for leaving the door standing open. Palmer called out "Very sorry, sir," but he shrugged his shoulders, and Henslow says, "I fancy Mr Dean's mistaken. I closed the door behind me, but he's a little upset." Then Palmer says, "Why, where's Worby?" and they saw him sitting on the step and went up to him. He was recovering himself, it seemed, and wiping his forehead, and Palmer helped him up on to his legs, as I was glad to see.

'They were too far off for me to hear what they said, but my father pointed to the north door in the aisle, and Palmer and Henslow both of them looked very surprised and scared. After a bit, my father and Henslow went out of the church, and the others made what haste they could to put the slab back and plaster it in. And about as the clock struck twelve the Cathedral was opened again and us boys made the best of our way home.

'I was in a great taking to know what it was had given my poor father such a turn, and when I got in and found him sitting in his chair taking a glass of spirits, and my mother standing looking anxious at him, I couldn't keep from bursting out and making confession where I'd been. But he didn't seem to take on, not in the way of losing his temper. "You was there, was you? Well, did you see it?" "I saw everything, father," I said, "except when the noise came." "Did you see what it was knocked the Dean over?" he says, "that what come out of the monument? You didn't? Well, that's a mercy." "Why, what was it, father?" I said. "Come, you must have seen it," he says. "*Didn't* you see? A thing like a man, all over hair, and two great eyes to it?"

'Well, that was all I could get out of him that time, and later on he seemed as if he was ashamed of being so frightened, and he used to put me off when I asked him about it. But years after when I was got to be a grown man, we had more talk now and again on the matter, and he always said the same thing. "Black it was," he'd say, "and a mass of hair, and two legs, and the light caught on its eyes."

'Well, that's the tale of that tomb, Mr Lake; it's one we don't tell to our visitors, and I should be obliged to you not to make any use of it till I'm out of the way. I doubt Mr Evans'll feel the same as I do, if you ask him.'

This proved to be the case. But over twenty years have passed by, and the grass is growing over both Worby and Evans; so Mr Lake felt no difficulty about communicating his notes – taken in 1890 – to me. He accompanied them with a sketch of the tomb and a copy of the short inscription on the metal cross which was affixed at the expense of Dr Lyall to the centre of the northern side. It was from the Vulgate of Isaiah xxiv., and consisted merely of the three words –

IBI CUBAVIT LAMIA.

CASTING THE RUNES

'April 15th, 190—.

DEAR SIR,

I am requested by the Council of the — Association to return to you the draft of a paper on *The Truth of Alchemy*, which you have been good enough to offer to read at our forthcoming meeting, and to inform you that the Council do not see their way to including it in the programme.

I am,

Yours faithfully,
— Secretary.'

'April 18th.

DEAR SIR,

I am sorry to say that my engagements do not permit of my affording you an interview on the subject of your proposed paper. Nor do our laws allow of your discussing the matter with a Committee of our Council, as you suggest. Please allow me to assure you that the fullest consideration was given to the draft which you submitted, and that it was not declined without having been referred to the judgment of a most competent authority. No personal question (it can hardly be necessary for me to add) can have had the slightest influence on the decision of the Council.

Believe me (ut supra).'

'April 20th.

The Secretary of the Association begs respectfully to inform Mr Karswell that it is impossible for him to communicate the name of any person or persons to whom the draft of Mr Karswell's paper may have been submitted; and further desires to intimate that he cannot undertake to reply to any further letters on this subject.'

*

"And who *is* Mr Karswell?" inquired the Secretary's wife. She had called at his office, and (perhaps unwarrantably) had picked up the last of these three letters, which the typist has just brought in.

"Why, my dear, just at present Mr Karswell is a very angry man. But I don't know much about him otherwise, except that he is a person of wealth, his address is Lufford Abbey, Warwickshire, and he's an alchemist, apparently, and wants to tell us all about it; and that's about all – except that I don't want to meet him for the next week or two. Now, if you're ready to leave this place, I am."

"What have you been doing to make him angry?" asked Mrs Secretary.

"The usual thing, my dear, the usual thing: he sent in a draft of a paper he wanted to read at the next meeting, and we referred it to Edward Dunning – about the only man in England who knows about these things – and he said it was perfectly hopeless, so we declined it. So Karswell has been pelting me with letters ever since. The last thing he wanted was the name of the man we referred his nonsense to; you saw my answer to that. But don't you say anything about it, for goodness' sake."

"I should think not, indeed. Did I ever do such a thing? I do hope, though, he won't get to know that it was poor Mr Dunning."

"Poor Mr Dunning? I don't know why you call him that; he's a very happy man, is Dunning. Lots of hobbies and a comfortable home, and all his time to himself."

"I only meant I should be sorry for him if this man got hold of his name, and came and bothered him."

"Oh, ah! yes, I daresay he would be poor Mr Dunning then."

*

The Secretary and his wife were lunching out, and the friends to whose house they were bound were Warwickshire people. So Mrs Secretary had already settled it in her own mind that she would question them judiciously about Mr Karswell. But she was saved the trouble of leading up to the subject, for the hostess said to the host, before many minutes had passed, "I saw the Abbot of Lufford this morning." The host whistled. "*Did* you? What in the world brings him up to town?" "Goodness knows; he was coming out of the British Museum gate as I drove past." It was not unnatural that Mrs Secretary should inquire whether this was a real Abbot who was being spoken of. "Oh no, my dear: only a neighbour of ours in the country who bought Lufford Abbey a few years ago. His real name is Karswell." "Is he a friend of yours?" asked Mr Secretary, with a private wink to his wife. The question let loose a torrent of declamation. There was really nothing to be said for Mr Karswell. Nobody knew what he did with himself: his servants were a horrible set of people; he had invented a new religion for himself, and practised no one could tell what appalling rites; he was very easily offended, and never forgave anybody: he had a dreadful face (so the lady insisted, her husband somewhat demurring); he never did a kind action, and whatever influence he did exert was mischievous. "Do the poor man justice, dear," the husband interrupted. "You forget the treat he gave the school children." "Forget it, indeed! But I'm glad you mentioned it, because it gives an idea of the man. Now, Florence, listen to this. The first winter he was at Lufford this delightful neighbour of ours wrote to the clergyman of his parish (he's not ours, but we know him very well) and offered to show the school children some magic-lantern slides. He said he had some new kinds, which he thought would interest them. Well, the clergyman was rather surprised, because Mr Karswell had shown himself inclined to be unpleasant to the children – complaining of their trespassing, or something of the sort; but of course he accepted, and the evening was fixed, and our friend went himself to see that everything went right. He said he never had been so thankful for anything as that his own children were all prevented from being there: they were at a children's party at our house, as a matter of fact. Because this Mr Karswell had evidently set out with the intention of frightening these poor village children out of their wits, and I do believe, if he had been allowed to go on, he would actually have done so. He began with some comparatively mild things. Red Riding Hood was one, and even then, Mr Farrer said, the wolf was so dreadful that several of the smaller children had to be taken out: and he said Mr Karswell began the story by producing a noise like a wolf howling in the distance, which was the most gruesome thing he had ever heard. All the slides he showed, Mr Farrer said, were most clever; they were absolutely realistic, and where he had got them or how he worked them he could not imagine. Well, the show went on, and the stories kept on becoming a little more terrifying each time, and the children were mesmerised into complete silence. At last he produced a series which represented a little boy passing through his own park – Lufford, I mean – in the evening. Every child in the room could recognise the place from the pictures. And this poor boy was followed, and at last pursued and overtaken, and either torn in pieces or somehow made away with, by a horrible hopping creature in white, which you saw first dodging about among the trees, and gradually it appeared more and more plainly. Mr Farrer said it gave him one of the worst nightmares he ever remembered, and what it must have meant to the children doesn't bear thinking of. Of course this was too much, and he spoke very sharply indeed to Mr Karswell, and said it couldn't go on. All *he* said was: 'Oh, you think it's time to bring our little show to an end and send them home to their beds? *Very* well!' and then, if you please, he switched on another slide, which showed a great mass of snakes, centipedes, and disgusting creatures with wings, and somehow or other he made it seem as if they were climbing out of the picture and getting in amongst the audience; and this was accompanied by a sort of dry rustling noise which sent the children nearly mad, and of course they stampeded. A good many of them were rather hurt in getting out of the room, and I don't suppose one of them closed an eye that night. There was the most dreadful trouble in the village afterwards. Of course the mothers threw a good part of the blame on poor Mr Farrer, and, if they could have got past the gates, I believe the fathers would have broken every window in the Abbey. Well, now, that's Mr Karswell: that's the Abbot of Lufford, my dear, and you can imagine how we covet *his* society."

"Yes, I think he has all the possibilities of a distinguished criminal, has Karswell," said the host. "I should be sorry for anyone who got into his bad books."

"Is he the man, or am I mixing him up with someone else?" asked the Secretary (who for some minutes had been wearing the frown of the man who is trying to recollect something). "Is he the man who brought out a *History of Witchcraft* some time back – ten years or more?"

"That's the man; do you remember the reviews of it?"

"Certainly I do; and what's equally to the point, I knew the author of the most incisive of the lot.

So did you: you must remember John Harrington; he was at John's in our time."

"Oh, very well indeed, though I don't think I saw or heard anything of him between the time I went down and the day I read the account of the inquest on him."

"Inquest?" said one of the ladies. "What has happened to him?"

"Why, what happened was that he fell out of a tree and broke his neck. But the puzzle was, what could have induced him to get up there. It was a mysterious business, I must say. Here was this man – not an athletic fellow, was he? and with no eccentric twist about him that was ever noticed – walking home along a country road late in the evening – no tramps about – well known and liked in the place – and he suddenly begins to run like mad, loses his hat and stick, and finally shins up a tree – quite a difficult tree – growing in the hedgerow: a dead branch gives way, and he comes down with it and breaks his neck, and there he's found next morning with the most dreadful face of fear on him that could be imagined. It was pretty evident, of course, that he had been chased by something, and people talked of savage dogs, and beasts escaped out of menageries; but there was nothing to be made of that. That was in '89, and I believe his brother Henry (whom I remember as well at Cambridge, but *you* probably don't) has been trying to get on the track of an explanation ever since. He, of course, insists there was malice in it, but I don't know. It's difficult to see how it could have come in."

After a time the talk reverted to the *History of Witchcraft*. "Did you ever look into it?" asked the host.

"Yes, I did," said the Secretary. "I went so far as to read it."

"Was it as bad as it was made out to be?"

"Oh, in point of style and form, quite hopeless. It deserved all the pulverising it got. But, besides that, it was an evil book. The man believed every word of what he was saying, and I'm very much mistaken if he hadn't tried the greater part of his receipts."

"Well, I only remember Harrington's review of it, and I must say if I'd been the author it would have quenched my literary ambition for good. I should never have held up my head again."

"It hasn't had that effect in the present case. But come, it's half-past three; I must be off."

On the way home the Secretary's wife said, "I do hope that horrible man won't find out that Mr Dunning had anything to do with the rejection of his paper." "I don't think there's much chance of that," said the Secretary. "Dunning won't mention it himself, for these matters are confidential, and none of us will for the same reason. Karswell won't know his name, for Dunning hasn't published anything on the same subject yet. The only danger is that Karswell might find out, if he was to ask the British Museum people who was in the habit of consulting alchemical manuscripts: I can't very well tell them not to mention Dunning, can I? It would set them talking at once. Let's hope it won't occur to him."

However, Mr Karswell was an astute man.

*

This much is in the way of prologue. On an evening rather later in the same week, Mr Edward Dunning was returning from the British Museum, where he had been engaged in Research, to the comfortable house in a suburb where he lived alone, tended by two excellent women who had been long with him. There is nothing to be added by way of description of him to what we have heard already. Let us follow him as he takes his sober course homewards.

A train took him to within a mile or two of his house, and an electric tram a stage further. The line ended at a point some three hundred yards from his front door. He had had enough of reading when he got into the car, and indeed the light was not such as to allow him to do more than study the advertisements on the panes of glass that faced him as he sat. As was not unnatural, the advertisements in this particular line of cars were objects of his frequent contemplation, and, with the possible exception, of the brilliant and convincing dialogue between Mr Lamplough and an eminent K.C. on the subject of Pyretic Saline, none of them afforded much scope to his imagination. I am wrong: there was one at the corner of the car furthest from him which did not seem familiar. It was in blue letters on a yellow ground, and all that he could read of it was a name – John Harrington – and something like a date. It could be of no interest to him to know more; but for all that, as the car emptied, he was just curious enough to move along the seat until he could read it well. He felt to a slight extent repaid for his trouble; the advertisement was *not* of the usual type. It ran thus: "In memory of John Harrington, F.S.A., of The Laurels, Ashbrooke. Died Sept. 18th, 1889. Three months were allowed."

The car stopped. Mr Dunning, still contemplating the blue letters on the yellow ground, had to be stimulated to rise by a word from the conductor. "I beg your pardon," he said, "I was looking at that advertisement; it's a very odd one, isn't it?" The conductor read it slowly. "Well, my word," he said, "I never see that one before. Well, that is a cure, ain't it? Some one bin up to their jokes 'ere, I should think." He got out a duster and applied it, not without saliva, to the pane and then to the outside. "No," he said, returning, "that ain't no transfer; seems to me as if it was reg'lar *in* the glass, what I mean in the substance, as you may say. Don't you think so, sir?" Mr Dunning examined it and rubbed it with his glove, and agreed. "Who looks after these advertisements, and gives leave for them to be put up? I wish you would inquire. I will just take a note of the words." At this moment there came a call from the driver: "Look alive, George, time's up." "All right, all right; there's somethink else what's up at this end. You come and look at this 'ere glass." "What's gorn with the glass?" said the driver, approaching. "Well, and oo's 'Arrington? What's it all about?" "I was just asking who was responsible for putting the advertisements up in your cars, and saying it would be as well to make some inquiry about this one." "Well, sir, that's all done at the Company's orfice, that work is: it's our Mr Timms, I believe, looks into that. When we put up tonight I'll leave word, and per'aps I'll be able to tell you tomorrer if you 'appen to be coming this way."

This was all that passed that evening. Mr Dunning did just go to the trouble of looking up Ashbrooke, and found that it was in Warwickshire.

Next day he went to town again. The car (it was the same car) was too full in the morning to allow of his getting a word with the conductor: he could only be sure that the curious advertisement had been made away with. The close of the day brought a further element of mystery into the transaction. He had missed the tram, or else preferred walking home, but at a rather late hour, while he was at work in his study, one of the maids came to say that two men from the tramways was very anxious to speak to him. This was a reminder of the advertisement, which he had, he says, nearly forgotten. He had the men in –

they were the conductor and driver of the car – and when the matter of refreshment had been attended to, asked what Mr Timms had had to say about the advertisement. "Well sir, that's what we took the liberty to step round about," said the conductor. "Mr Timm's 'e give William 'ere the rough side of his tongue about that: 'cordin' to 'im there warn't no advertisement of that description sent in, nor ordered, nor paid for, nor put up, nor nothink, let alone not bein' there, and we was playing the fool takin' up his time. 'Well,' I says, 'if that's the case, all I ask of you, Mr Timms,' I says, 'is to take and look at it for yourself,' I says. 'Of course if it ain't there,' I says, 'you may take and call me what you like.' 'Right,' he says, 'I will': and we went straight off. Now, I leave it to you, sir, if that ad., as we term 'em, with 'Arrington on it warn't as plain as ever you see anything – blue letters on yeller glass, and as I says at the time, and you borne me out, reg'lar in the glass, because, if you remember, you recollect of me swabbing it with my duster." "To be sure I do, quite clearly – well?" "You may say well, I don't think. Mr Timms he gets in that car with a light – no, he telled William to 'old the light outside. 'Now,' he says, 'where's your precious ad. what we've 'eard so much about?' ''Ere it is,' I says, 'Mr Timms,' and I laid my 'and on it." The conductor paused.

"Well," said Mr Dunning, "it was gone, I suppose. Broken?"

"Broke! – not it. There warn't, if you'll believe me, no more trace of them letters – blue letters they was – on that piece o' glass, than – well, it's no good *me* talkin'. *I* never see such a thing. I leave it to William here if – but there, as I says, where's the benefit in me going on about it?"

"And what did Mr Timms say?"

"Why'e did what I give 'im leave to – called us

pretty much anything he liked, and I don't know as I blame him so much neither. But what we thought, William and me did, was as we seen you take down a bit of a note about that – well, that letterin'—"

"I certainly did that, and I have it now. Did you wish me to speak to Mr Timms myself, and show it to him? Was that what you came in about?"

"There, didn't I say as much?" said William. "Deal with a gent if you can get on the track of one, that's my word. Now perhaps, George, you'll allow as I ain't took you very far wrong to-night."

"Very well, William, very well; no need for you to go on as if you'd 'ad to frog's-march me 'ere. I come quiet, didn't I? All the same for that, we 'adn't ought to take up your time this way, sir; but if it so 'appened you could find time to step round to the Company's orfice in the morning and tell Mr Timms what you seen for yourself, we should lay under a very 'igh obligation to you for the trouble. You see it ain't bein' called – well, one thing and another, as we mind, but if they got it into their 'ead at the orfice as we seen things as warn't there, why, one thing leads to another, and where we should be a twelvemunce 'ence – well, you can understand what I mean."

Amid further elucidations of the proposition, George, conducted by William, left the room.

The incredulity of Mr Timms (who had a nodding acquaintance with Mr Dunning) was greatly modified on the following day by what the latter could tell and show him; and any bad mark that might have been attached to the names of William and George was not suffered to remain on the Company's books; but explanation there was none.

Mr Dunning's interest in the matter was kept alive by an incident of the following afternoon. He was walking from his club to the train, and he noticed some way ahead a man with a handful of leaflets such as are distributed to passers-by by agents of enterprising firms. This agent had not chosen a very crowded street for his operations: in fact, Mr Dunning did not see him get rid of a single leaflet before he himself reached the spot. One was thrust into his hand as he passed: the hand that gave it touched his, and he experienced a sort of little shock as it did so. It seemed unnaturally rough and hot. He looked in passing at the giver, but the impression he got was so unclear that, however much he tried to reckon it up subsequently, nothing would come. He was walking quickly, and as he went on glanced at the paper. It was a blue one. The name of Harrington in large capitals caught his eye. He stopped, startled, and felt for his glasses. The next instant the leaflet was twitched out of his hand by a man who hurried past, and was irrecoverably gone. He ran back a few paces, but where was the passer-by? and where the distributor?

It was in a somewhat pensive frame of mind that Mr Dunning passed on the following day into the Select Manuscript Room of the British Museum, and filled up tickets for Harley 3586, and some other volumes. After a few minutes they were brought to him, and he was settling the one he wanted first upon the desk, when he thought he heard his own name whispered behind him. He turned round hastily, and, in doing so, brushed his little portfolio of loose papers on to the floor. He saw no one he recognised except one of the staff in charge of the room, who nodded to him, and he proceeded to pick up his papers. He thought he had them all, and was turning to begin work, when a stout gentleman at the table behind him, who was just rising to leave, and had collected his own belongings, touched him on the shoulder, saying, "May I give you this? I think it should be yours," and handed him a missing quire. "It is mine, thank you," said Mr Dunning. In another moment the man had left the room. Upon finishing his work for the afternoon, Mr Dunning had some conversation with the assistant in charge, and took occasion to ask who the stout gentleman was. "Oh, he's a man named Karswell," said the assistant, "he was asking me a week ago who were the great authorities on alchemy, and of course I told him you were the only one in the country. I'll see if I can't catch him: he'd like to meet you, I'm sure."

"For heaven's sake don't dream of it!" said Mr Dunning, "I'm particularly anxious to avoid him."

"Oh! very well," said the assistant, "he doesn't come here often: I daresay you won't meet him."

More than once on the way home that day Mr Dunning confessed to himself that he did not look forward with his usual cheerfulness to a solitary evening. It seemed to him that something ill-defined and impalpable had stepped in between him and his fellow-men – had taken him in charge, as it were. He wanted to sit close up to his neighbours in the train and in the tram, but as luck would have it both train and car were markedly empty. The conductor George was thoughtful and appeared to be absorbed in calculations as to the number of passengers. On arriving at his house he found Dr Watson, his medical man, on his doorstep. "I've had to upset your household arrangements, I'm sorry to say, Dunning. Both your servants hors de combat. In fact, I've had to send them to the Nursing Home."

"Good heavens! what's the matter?"

"It's something like ptomaine poisoning, I should think: you've not suffered yourself, I can see, or you wouldn't be walking about. I think they'll pull through all right."

"Dear, dear! Have you any idea what brought it on?"

"Well, they tell me they bought some shellfish from a hawker at their dinnertime. It's odd. I've made inquiries, but I can't find that any hawker has been to other houses in the street. I couldn't send word to you; they won't be back for a bit yet. You come and dine with me tonight, anyhow, and we can make arrangements for going on. Eight o'clock. Don't be too anxious."

The solitary evening was thus obviated; at the expense of some distress and inconvenience, it is true. Mr Dunning spent the time pleasantly enough with the doctor (a rather recent settler), and returned to his lonely home at about 11.30. The night he passed is not one on which he looks back with any satisfaction. He was in bed and the light was out. He was wondering if the charwoman would come early enough to get him hot water next morning, when he heard the unmistakable sound of his study door opening. No step followed it on the passage floor, but the sound must mean mischief, for he knew that he had shut the door that evening after putting his papers away in his desk. It was rather shame than courage that induced him to slip out into the passage and lean over the banister in his nightgown, listening. No light was visible; no further sound came: only a gust of warm, or even hot air played for an instant round his shins. He went back and decided to lock himself into his room. There was more unpleasantness, however. Either an economical suburban company had decided that their light would not be required in the small hours, and had stopped working, or else something was wrong with the meter; the effect was in any case that the electric light was off. The obvious course was to find a match, and also to consult his watch: he might as well know how many hours of discomfort awaited him. So he put his hand into the well-known nook under the pillow: only, it did not get so far. What he touched was, according to his account, a mouth, with teeth, and with hair about it, and, he declares, not the mouth of a human being. I do not think it is any use to guess what he said or did; but he was in a spare room with the door locked and his ear to it before he was clearly conscious again. And there he spent the rest of a most miserable night, looking every moment for some fumbling at the door: but nothing came.

The venturing back to his own room in the morning was attended with many listenings and quiverings. The door stood open, fortunately, and the blinds were up (the servants had been out of the house before the hour of drawing them down); there was, to be short, no trace of an inhabitant. The watch, too, was in its usual place; nothing was disturbed, only the wardrobe door had swung open, in accordance with its confirmed habit. A ring at the back door now announced the charwoman, who had been ordered the night before, and nerved Mr Dunning, after letting her in, to continue his search in other parts of the house. It was equally fruitless.

The day thus begun, went on dismally enough. He dared not go to the Museum: in spite of what the assistant had said, Karswell might turn up there, and Dunning felt he could not cope with a probably hostile stranger. His own house was odious; he hated sponging on the doctor. He spent some little time in a call at the Nursing Home, where he was slightly cheered by a good report of his housekeeper and maid. Towards lunchtime he betook himself to his club, again experiencing a gleam of satisfaction at seeing the Secretary of the Association. At luncheon Dunning told his friend the more material of his woes, but could not bring himself to speak of those that weighed most heavily on his spirits. "My poor dear man," said the Secretary, "what an upset! Look here: we're alone at home, absolutely. You must put up with us. Yes! no excuse: send your things in this afternoon." Dunning was unable to stand out: he was, in truth, becoming acutely anxious, as the hours went on, as to what that night might have waiting for him. He was almost happy as he hurried home to pack up.

His friends, when they had time to take stock of him, were rather shocked at his lorn appearance, and did their best to keep him up to the mark. Not altogether without success: but, when the two men were smoking alone later, Dunning became dull again. Suddenly he said, "Gayton, I believe that alchemist man knows it was I who got his paper rejected." Gayton whistled. "What makes you think that?" he said. Dunning told of his conversation with the Museum assistant, and Gayton could only agree that the guess seemed likely to be correct. "Not that I care much," Dunning went on, "only it might be a nuisance if we were to meet. He's a bad-tempered party, I imagine." Conversation dropped again; Gayton became more and more strongly impressed with the desolateness that came over Dunning's face and bearing, and finally – though with a considerable effort – he asked him point-blank whether something serious was not bothering him. Dunning gave an exclamation of relief. "I was perishing to get it off my mind," he said. "Do you know anything about a man named John Harrington?" Gayton was thoroughly startled, and at the moment could only ask why. Then the complete story of Dunning's experiences came out – what had happened in the tramcar, in his own house, and in the street, the troubling of spirit that had crept over him, and still held him; and he ended with the question he had begun with. Gayton was at a loss how to answer him. To tell the story of Harrington's end would perhaps be right; only, Dunning was in a nervous state, the story was a grim one, and he could not help asking himself whether there were not a connecting link between these two cases, in the person of Karswell. It was a difficult concession for a scientific man, but it could be eased by the phrase "hypnotic suggestion". In the end he decided that his answer tonight should be guarded; he would talk the situation over with his wife. So he said that he had known Harrington at Cambridge, and believe he had died suddenly in 1889, adding a few details about the man and his published work. He did talk over the matter with Mrs Gayton, and, as he had anticipated, she leapt at once to the conclusion which had been hovering before him. It was she who reminded him of the surviving brother, Henry Harrington, and she also who suggested that he might be got hold of by means of their hosts of the day before. "He might be a hopeless crank," objected Gayton. "That could be ascertained from the Bennetts, who knew him," Mrs Gayton retorted; and she undertook to see the Bennetts the very next day.

*

It is not necessary to tell in further detail the steps by which Henry Harrington and Dunning were brought together.

*

The next scene that requires to be narrated is a conversation that took place between the two. Dunning had told Harrington of the strange ways in which the dead man's name had been brought before him, and had said something, besides, of his own subsequent experiences. Then he had asked if Harrington was disposed, in return, to recall any of the circumstances connected with his brother's death. It is not necessary to dwell on Harrington's surprise at what he had heard: but his reply was readily given.

"John," he said, "was in a very odd state, undeniably, from time to time, during some weeks before, though not immediately before, the catastrophe. There were several things – the principal notion he had was that he thought he was being followed. No doubt he was an impressionable man, but he never had had such fancies as this before. I cannot get it out of my mind that there was ill-will at work, and what you tell me about yourself reminds me very much of my brother. Can you think of any possible connecting link?"

"There is just one that has been taking shape vaguely in my mind. I've been told that your brother reviewed a book very severely not long before he died, and just lately I have happened to cross the path of the man who wrote that book in a way he would resent."

"Don't tell me the man was called Karswell."

"Why not? that is exactly his name."

Henry Harrington leant back. "That is final to my mind. Now I must explain further. From something he said, I feel sure that my brother John was beginning to believe – very much against his will – that Karswell was at the bottom of his trouble. I want to tell you what seems to me to have a bearing on this situation. My brother was a great musician, and used to run up to concerts in town. He came back, three months before he died, from one of these, and gave me his programme to look at – an analytical programme: he always kept them. 'I nearly missed this one' he said. 'I suppose I must have dropped it: anyhow I was looking for it under my seat and in my pockets and so on, and my neighbour offered me his: said 'might he give it me, he had no further use for it,' and he went away just afterwards. I don't know who he was – a stout, clean-shaven man. I should have been sorry to miss it; of course I could have bought another, but this cost me nothing." At another time he told me that he had been very uncomfortable both on the way to his hotel and during the night. I piece things together now in thinking it over. Then, not very long after, he was going over these programmes, putting them in order to have them bound up, and in this particular one (which by the way I had hardly glanced at), he found quite near the beginning a strip of paper with some very odd writing on it in red and black – most carefully done – it looked to me more like Runic letters than anything else. "Why," he said, "this must belong to my fat neighbour. It looks as if it might be worth returning to him; it may be a copy of something; evidently someone has taken trouble over it. How can I find his address?" We talked it over for a little and agreed that it wasn't worth advertising about, and that my brother had better look out for the man at the next concert, to which he was going very soon. The paper was lying on the book and we were both by the fire; it was a cold, windy summer evening. I suppose the door blew open, though I didn't notice it: at any rate a gust – a warm gust it was – came quite suddenly between us, took the paper and blew it straight into the fire: it was light, thin paper, and flared and went up the chimney in a single ash. 'Well,' I said, 'you can't give it back now.' He said nothing for a minute: then rather crossly, 'No, I can't; but why you should keep on saying so I don't know.' I remarked that I didn't say it more than once. 'Not more than four times, you mean,' was all he said. I remember all that very clearly, without any good reason; and now to come to the point. I don't know if you looked at that book of Karswell's which my unfortunate brother reviewed. It's not likely that you should: but I did, both before his death and after it. The first time we made game of it together. It was written in no style at all – split infinitives, and every sort of thing that makes an Oxford gorge rise. Then there was nothing that the man didn't swallow: mixing up classical myths, and stories out of the *Golden Legend* with reports of savage customs of today – all very proper, no doubt, if you know how to use them, but he didn't: he seemed to put the *Golden Legend* and the *Golden Bough* exactly on a par, and to believe both: a pitiable exhibition, in short. Well, after the misfortune, I looked over the book again. It was no better than before, but the impression which it left this time on my mind was different. I suspected – as I told you – that Karswell had borne ill-will to my brother – even that he was in some way responsible for what had happened – and now his book seemed to me to be a very sinister performance indeed. One chapter in particular struck me, in which he spoke of 'casting the Runes' on people, either for the purpose of gaining their affection or of getting them out of the way – perhaps more especially the latter: he spoke of all this in a way that really seemed to me to imply actual knowledge. I've not time to go into details, but the upshot is that I am pretty sure from information received that the civil man at the concert was Karswell: I suspect – I more than suspect – that the paper was of importance: and I do believe that if my brother had been able to give it back, he might have been alive now. Therefore, it occurs to me to ask you whether you have anything to put beside what I have told you."

By way of answer, Dunning had the episode in the Manuscript Room at the British Museum to relate. "Then he did actually hand you some papers; have you examined them? No? because we must, if you'll allow it, look at them at once, and very carefully."

They went to the still empty house – empty, for the two servants were not yet able to return to work. Dunning's portfolio of papers was gathering dust on the writing-table. In it were the quires of small-sized scribbling paper which he used for his transcripts: and from one of these, as he took it up, there slipped and fluttered out into the room with uncanny quickness, a strip of thin light paper. The window was open, but Harrington slammed it to, just in time to intercept the paper, which he caught. "I thought so," he said; "it might be the identical thing that was given to my brother. You have to look out, Dunning; this may mean something quite serious for you."

A long consultation took place. The paper was narrowly examined. As Harrington had said, the characters on it were more like Runes than anything else, but not decipherable by either man, and both hesitated to copy them, for fear, as they confessed, of perpetuating whatever evil purpose they might conceal. So it has remained impossible (if I may anticipate a little) to ascertain what was conveyed in this curious message or commission. Both Dunning and Harrington are firmly convinced that it had the effect of bringing its possessors into very undesirable company. That it must be returned to the source whence it came they were agreed, and further, that the only safe and certain way was that of personal service; and here contrivance would be necessary, for Dunning was known by sight to Karswell. He must, for one thing, alter his appearance by shaving his beard. But then might not the blow fall first? Harrington thought they could time it. He knew the date of the concert at which the 'black spot' had been put on his brother: it was June 18th. The death had followed on Sept. 18th. Dunning reminded him that three months had been mentioned on the inscription on the car-window. "Perhaps," he added, with a cheerless laugh, "mine may be a bill at three months too. I believe I can fix it by my diary. Yes, April 23rd was the day at the Museum; that brings us to July 23rd. Now, you know, it becomes extremely important to me to know anything you will tell me about the progress of your brother's trouble, if it is possible for you to speak of it." "Of course. Well, the sense of being watched whenever he was alone was the most distressing thing to him. After a time I took to sleeping in his room, and he was the better for that: still, he talked a great deal in his sleep. What about? Is it wise to dwell on that, at least before things are straightened out? I think not, but I can tell you this: two things came for him by post during those weeks, both with a London postmark, and addressed in a commercial hand. One was a woodcut of Bewick's, roughly torn out of the page: one which shows a moonlit road and a man walking along it, followed by an awful demon creature. Under it were written the lines out of the 'Ancient Mariner' (which I suppose the cut illustrates) about one who, having once looked round—

"Walks on, and turns no more his head,
Because he knows a grisly fiend doth close behind
  him tread."

The other was a calendar, such as tradesmen often send. My brother paid no attention to this, but I looked at it after his death, and found that everything after Sept. 18 had been torn out. You may be surprised at his having gone out alone the evening he was killed, but the fact is that during the last ten days or so of his life he had been quite free from the sense of being followed or watched."

The end of the consultation was this. Harrington, who knew a neighbour of Karswell's, thought he saw a way of keeping a watch on his movements. It would be Dunning's part to be in readiness to try to cross Karswell's path at any moment, to keep the paper safe and in a place of ready access.

They parted. The next weeks were no doubt a severe strain upon Dunning's nerves: the intangible barrier which had seemed to rise about him on the day when he received the paper, gradually developed into a brooding blackness that cut him off from all the means of escape to which one might have thought he would resort. No one was at hand who was likely to suggest them to him, and he seemed robbed of all initiative. He waited with inexpressible anxiety as May, June, and early July passed on, for a mandate from Harrington. But all this time Karswell remained immovable at Lufford.

At last, in less than a week before the date he had come to look upon as the end of his earthly activities, came a telegram: "Leaves Victoria by boat train Thursday night. Do not miss. I come to you tonight. Harrington."

He arrived accordingly, and they concocted plans. The train left Victoria at nine and its last stop before Dover was Croydon West. Harrington would mark down Karswell at Victoria, and look out for Dunning at Croydon, calling to him if need were by a name agreed upon. Dunning, disguised as far as might be, was to have no label or initials on any hand luggage, and must at all costs have the paper with him.

Dunning's suspense as he waited on the Croydon platform I need not attempt to describe. His sense of danger during the last days had only been sharpened by the fact that the cloud about him had perceptibly been lighter; but relief was an ominous symptom, and, if Karswell eluded him now, hope was gone: and there were so many chances of that. The rumour of the journey might be itself a device. The twenty minutes in which he paced the platform and persecuted every porter with inquiries as to the boat train were as bitter as any he had spent. Still, the train came, and Harrington was at the window. It was important, of course, that there should be no recognition: so Dunning got in at the further end of the corridor carriage, and only gradually made his way to the compartment where Harrington and Karswell were. He was pleased, on the whole, to see that the train was far from full.

Karswell was on the alert, but gave no sign of recognition. Dunning took the seat not immediately facing him, and attempted, vainly at first, then with increasing command of his faculties, to reckon the possibilities of making the desired transfer. Opposite to Karswell, and next to Dunning, was a heap of Karswell's coats on the seat. It would be of no use to slip the paper into these — he would not be safe, or would not feel so, unless in some way it could be proffered by him and accepted by the other. There was a handbag, open, and with papers in it. Could he manage to conceal this (so that perhaps Karswell might leave the carriage without it), and then find and give it to him? This was the plan that suggested itself. If he could only have counselled with Harrington! but that could not be. The minutes went on. More than once Karswell rose and went out into the corridor. The second time Dunning was on the point of attempting to make the bag fall off the seat, but he caught Harrington's eye, and read in it a warning. Karswell, from the corridor, was watching: probably to see if the two men recognised each other. He returned, but was evidently restless: and, when he rose the third time, hope dawned, for something did slip off his seat and fall with hardly a sound to the floor.

Karswell went out once more, and passed out of range of the corridor window. Dunning picked up what had fallen, and saw that the key was in his hands in the form of one of Cook's ticket-cases, with tickets in it. These cases have a pocket in the cover, and within very few seconds the paper of which we have heard was in the pocket of this one. To make the operation more secure, Harrington stood in the doorway of the compartment and fiddled with the blind. It was done, and done at the right time, for the train was now slowing down towards Dover.

In a moment more Karswell re-entered the compartment. As he did so, Dunning, managing, he knew not how, to suppress the tremble in his voice, handed him the ticket-case, saying, "May I give you this, sir? I believe it is yours." After a brief glance at the ticket inside, Karswell uttered the hoped-for response, "Yes, it is; much obliged to you, sir," and he placed it in his breast pocket.

Even in the few moments that remained – moments of tense anxiety, for they knew not to what a premature finding of the paper might lead – both men noticed that the carriage seemed to darken about them and to grow warmer; that Karswell was fidgety and oppressed; that he drew the heap of loose coats near to him and cast it back as if it repelled him; and that he then sat upright and glanced anxiously at both. They, with sickening anxiety, busied themselves in collecting their belongings; but they both thought that Karswell was on the point of speaking when the train stopped at Dover Town. It was natural that in the short space between town and pier they should both go into the corridor.

At the pier they got out, but so empty was the train that they were forced to linger on the platform until Karswell should have passed ahead of them with his porter on the way to the boat, and only then was it safe for them to exchange a pressure of the hand and a word of concentrated congratulation. The effect upon Dunning was to make him almost faint. Harrington made him lean up against the wall, while he himself went forward a few yards within sight of the gangway to the boat, at which Karswell had now arrived. The man at the head of it examined his ticket, and, laden with coats, he passed down into the boat. Suddenly the official called after him, "You, sir, beg pardon, did the other gentleman show his ticket?" "What the devil do you mean by the other gentleman?" Karswell's snarling voice called back from the deck. The man bent over and looked at him. "The devil? Well, I don't know, I'm sure," Harrington heard him say to himself, and then aloud, "My mistake, sir; must have been your rugs! ask your pardon." And then, to a subordinate near him, "'Ad he got a dog with him, or what? Funny thing: I could 'a' swore 'e wasn't alone. Well, whatever it was, they'll 'ave to see to it aboard. She's off now. Another week and we shall be gettin' the 'oliday customers." In five minutes more there was nothing but the lessening lights of the boat, the long line of the Dover lamps, the night breeze, and the moon. ·

Long and long the two sat in their room at the Lord Warden. In spite of the removal of their greatest anxiety, they were oppressed with a doubt, not of the lightest. Had they been justified in sending a man to his death, as they believed they had? Ought they not to warn him, at least? "No," said Harrington; "if he is the murderer I think him, we have done no more than is just. Still, if you think it better – but how and where can you warn him?" "He was booked to Abbeville only," said Dunning. "I saw that. If I wired to the hotels there in Joanne's Guide, 'Examine your ticket-case, Dunning,' I should feel happier. This is the 21st: he will have a day. But I am afraid he has gone into the dark." So telegrams were left at the hotel office.

It is not clear whether these reached their destination, or whether, if they did, they were understood. All that is known is that, on the afternoon of the 23rd, an English traveller, examining the front of St Wulfram's Church at Abbeville, then under extensive repair, was struck on the head and instantly killed by a stone falling from the scaffold erected round the south-western tower, there being, as was clearly proved, no workman on the scaffold at that moment: and the traveller's paper identified him as Mr Karswell.

Only one detail shall be added. At Karswell's sale a set of Bewick, sold with all faults, was acquired by Harrington. The page with the woodcut of the traveller and the demon was, as he had expected, mutilated. Also, after a judicious interval, Harrington repeated to Dunning something of what he had heard his brother say in his sleep: but it was not long before Dunning stopped him.

COUNT MAGNUS

* * *

By what means the papers out of which I have made a connected story came into my hands is the last point which the reader will learn from these pages. But it is necessary to prefix to my extracts from them a statement of the form in which I possess them.

They consist, then, partly of a series of collections for a book of travels, such a volume as was a common product of the forties and fifties. Horace Marryat's *Journal of a Residence in Jutland and the Danish Isles* is a fair specimen of the class to which I allude. These books usually treated of some unfamiliar district on the Continent. They were illustrated with woodcuts or steel plates. They gave details of hotel accommodation, and of means of communication, such as we now expect to find in any well-regulated guidebook, and they dealt largely in reported conversations with intelligent foreigners, racy innkeepers and garrulous peasants. In a word, they were chatty.

Begun with the idea of furnishing material for such a book, my papers as they progressed assumed the character of a record of one single personal experience, and this record was continued up to the very eve, almost, of its termination.

The writer was a Mr. Wraxall. For my knowledge of him I have to depend entirely on the evidence his writings afford, and from these I deduce that he was a man past middle age, possessed of some private means, and very much alone in the world. He had, it seems, no settled abode in England, but was a denizen of hotels and boarding-houses. It is probable that he entertained the idea of settling down at some future time which never came; and I think it also likely that the Pantechnicon fire in the early seventies must have destroyed a great deal that would have thrown light on his antecedents, for he refers once or twice to property of his that was warehoused at that establishment.

It is further apparent that Mr. Wraxall had published a book, and that it treated of a holiday he had once taken in Brittany. More than this I cannot say about his work, because a diligent search in bibliographical works has convinced me that it must have appeared either anonymously or under a pseudonym.

As to his character, it is not difficult to form some superficial opinion. He must have been an intelligent and cultivated man. It seems that he was near being a Fellow of his college at Oxford – Brasenose, as I judge from the Calendar. His besetting fault was pretty clearly that of over-inquisitiveness, possibly a good fault in a traveller; certainly a fault for which this traveller paid dearly enough in the end.

On what proved to be his last expedition, he was plotting another book. Scandinavia, a region not widely known to Englishmen forty years ago, had struck him as an interesting field. He must have lighted on some old books of Swedish history or memoirs, and the idea had struck him that there was room for a book descriptive of travel in Sweden, interspersed with episodes from the history of some of the great Swedish families. He procured letters of introduction, therefore, to some persons of quality in Sweden, and set out thither in the early summer of 1863.

Of his travels in the North there is no need to speak, nor of his residence of some weeks in Stockholm. I need only mention that some *savant* resident there put him on the track of an important collection of family papers belonging to the proprietors of an ancient manor-house in Vestergothland, and obtained for him permission to examine them.

The manor-house, or *herrgård*, in question is to be called Råbäck (pronounced something like Roebeck), though that is not its name. It is one of the best buildings of its kind in all the country, and the picture of it in Dahlemberg's *Suecia antiqua et moderna*, engraved in 1964, shows it very much as the tourist may see it today. It was built soon after 1600, and is, roughly speaking, very much like an English house of that period in respect of material – red-brick with stone facings – and style. The man who built it was a scion of the great house of De la Gardie, and his descendants possess it still. De la Gardie is the name by which I will designate them when mention of them becomes necessary.

They received Mr. Wraxall with great kindness and courtesy, and pressed him to stay in the house as long as his researches lasted. But, preferring to be independent, and mistrusting his powers of conversing in Swedish, he settled himself at the village inn, which turned out quite sufficiently comfortable, at any rate during the summer months. This arrangement would entail a short walk daily to and from the manor-house of something under a mile. The house itself stood in a park, and was protected – we should say grown up – with large old timber. Near it you found the walled garden, and then entered a close wood fringing one of the small lakes with which the whole country is pitted. Then came the wall of the demesne, and you climbed a steep knoll – a knob of rock lightly covered with soil – and on the top of this stood the church, fenced in with tall dark trees. It was a curious building to English eyes. The nave and aisles were low, and filled with pews and galleries. In the western gallery stood the handsome old organ, gaily painted, and with silver pipes. The ceiling was flat, and had been adorned by a seventeenth-century artist with a strange and hideous 'Last Judgment', full of lurid flames, falling cities, burning ships, crying souls, and brown and smiling demons. Handsome brass coronae hung from the roof; the pulpit was like a doll's house, covered with little painted wooden cherubs and saints; a stand with three hour-glasses was hinged to the preacher's desk. Such sights as these may be seen in many a church in Sweden now, but what distinguished this one was an addition to the original building. At the eastern end of the north aisle the builder of the manor-house had erected a mausoleum for himself and his family. It was a largish eight-sided building, lighted by a series of oval windows, and it had a domed roof, topped by a kind of pumpkin-shaped object rising into a spire, a form in which Swedish architects greatly delighted. The roof was of copper externally, and was painted black, while the walls, in common with those of the church, were staringly white. To this mausoleum there was no access from the church. It had a portal and steps of its own on the northern side.

Past the churchyard the path to the village goes, and not more than three or four minutes bring you to the inn door.

On the first day of his stay at Råbäck Mr. Wraxall found the church door open, and made those notes of the interior which I have epitomized. Into the mausoleum, however, he could not make his way. He could by looking through the keyhole just descry that there were fine marble effigies and sarcophagi of copper, and a wealth of armorial ornament, which made him very anxious to spend some time in investigation.

The papers he had come to examine at the manor-house proved to be of just the kind he wanted for his book. There were family correspondence, journals and account-books of the earliest owners of the estate, very carefully kept and clearly written, full of amusing and picturesque detail. The first De la Gardie appeared in them as a strong and capable man. Shortly after the building of the mansion there had been a period of distress in the district, and the peasants had risen and attacked several châteaux and done some damage. The owner of Råbäck took a leading part in suppressing the trouble, and there was reference to executions of ringleaders and severe punishments inflicted with no sparing hand.

The portrait of this Magnus de la Gardie was one of the best in the house, and Mr. Wraxall studied it with no little interest after his day's work. He gives no detailed description of it, but I gather that the face impressed him rather by its power than by its beauty or goodness; in fact, he writes that Count Magnus was an almost phenomenally ugly man.

On this day Mr. Wraxall took his supper with the family, and walked back in the late but still bright evening.

'I must remember,' he writes, 'to ask the sexton if he can let me into the mausoleum at the church. He evidently has access to it himself, for I saw him tonight standing on the steps, and, as I thought, locking or unlocking the door.'

I find that early on the following day Mr. Wraxall had some conversation with his landlord. His setting it down at such length as he does surprised me at first; but I soon realized that the papers I was reading were, at least in their beginning, the materials for the book he was meditating, and that it was to have been one of those quasi-journalistic productions which admit of the introduction of an admixture of conversational matter.

His object, he says, was to find out whether any traditions of Count Magnus de la Gardie lingered on in the scenes of that gentleman's activity, and whether the popular estimate of him were favourable or not. He found that the Count was decidedly not a favourite. If his tenants came late to their work on the days which they owed to him as Lord of the Manor, they were set on the wooden horse, or flogged and branded in the manor-house yard. One or two cases there were of men who had occupied lands which encroached on the lord's domain, and whose houses had been mysteriously burnt on a winter's night, with the whole family inside. But what seemed to dwell on the innkeeper's mind most – for he returned to the subject more than once – was that the Count had been on the Black Pilgrimage, and had brought something or someone back with him.

You will naturally inquire, as Mr. Wraxall did, what the Black Pilgrimage may have been. But your curiosity on the point must remain unsatisfied for the time being, just as his did. The landlord was evidently unwilling to give a full answer, or indeed any answer, on the point, and, being called out for a moment, trotted off with obvious alacrity, only putting his head in at the door a few minutes afterwards to say that he was called away to Skara, and should not be back till evening.

So Mr. Wraxall had to go unsatisfied to his day's work at the manor-house. The papers on which he was just then engaged soon put his thoughts into another channel, for he had to occupy himself with glancing over the correspondence between Sophia Albertina in Stockholm and her married cousin Ulrica Leonora at Råbäck in the years 1705–1710. The letters were of exceptional interest from the light they threw upon the culture of that period in Sweden, as anyone can testify who has read the full edition of them in the publications of the Swedish Historical Manuscripts Commission.

In the afternoon he had done with these, and after returning the boxes in which they were kept to their places on the shelf, he proceeded, very naturally, to take down some of the volumes nearest to them, in order to determine which of them had best be his principal subject of investigation next day. The shelf he had hit upon was occupied mostly by a collection of account-books in the writing of the first Count Magnus. But one among them was not an account-book, but a book of alchemical and other tracts in another sixteenth-century hand. Not being very familiar with alchemical literature, Mr. Wraxall spends much space which he might have spared in setting out the names and beginnings of the various treatises: The book of the Phoenix, book of the Thirty Words, book of the Toad, book of Miriam, Turba philosophorum, and so forth; and then he announces with a good deal of circumstance, his delight at finding, on a leaf originally left blank near the middle of the book, some writing of Count Magnus himself headed 'Liber nigrae peregrinationis'. It is true that only a few lines were written, but there was quite enough to show that the landlord had that morning been referring to a belief at least as old as the time of Count Magnus, and probably shared by him. This is the English of what was written:

'If any man desires to obtain a long life, if he would obtain a faithful messenger and see the blood of his enemies, it is necessary that he should first go into the city of Chorazin, and there salute the prince. . . .' Here there was an erasure of one word, not very thoroughly done, so that Mr. Wraxall felt pretty sure that he was right in reading it as aëris ('of the air'). But there was no more of the text copied, only a line in Latin: 'Quaere reliqua hujus materiei inter secretioria' (See the rest of this matter among the more private things).

It could not be denied that this threw a rather lurid light upon the tastes and beliefs of the Count; but to Mr. Wraxall, separated from him by nearly three centuries, the thought that he might have added to his general forcefulness alchemy, and to alchemy something like magic, only made him a more picturesque figure; and when, after a rather prolonged contemplation of his picture in the hall, Mr. Wraxall set out on his homeward way, his mind was full of the thought of Count Magnus. He had no eyes for his surroundings, no perception of the evening scents of the woods or the evening light on the lake; and when all of a sudden he pulled up short, he was astonished to find himself already at the gate of the churchyard, and within a few minutes of his dinner. His eyes fell on the mausoleum.

'Ah,' he said, 'Count Magnus, there you are. I should dearly like to see you.'

'Like many solitary men,' he writes, 'I have a habit of talking to myself aloud; and, unlike some of the Greek and Latin particles, I do not expect an answer. Certainly, and perhaps fortunately in this case, there was neither voice nor any that regarded: only the woman who, I suppose, was cleaning up the church dropped some metallic object on the floor, whose clang startled me. Count Magnus, I think, sleeps sound enough.'

That same evening the landlord of the inn, who had heard Mr. Wraxall say that he wished to see the clerk or deacon (as he would be called in Sweden) of the parish, introduced him to that official in the inn parlour. A visit to the De la Gardie tomb-house was soon arranged for the next day, and a little general conversation ensued.

Mr. Wraxall, remembering that one function of Scandinavian deacons is to teach candidates for Confirmation, thought he would refresh his own memory on a Biblical point.

'Can you tell me,' he said, 'anything about Chorazin?'

The deacon seemed startled, but readily reminded him how that village had once been denounced.

'To be sure,' said Mr. Wraxall; 'it is, I suppose, quite a ruin now?'

'So I expect,' replied the deacon. 'I have heard some of our old priests say that Antichrist is to be born there; and there are tales—'

'Ah! what tales are those?' Mr. Wraxall put in.

'Tales, I was going to say, which I have forgotten,' said the deacon; and soon after that he said good night.

The landlord was now alone, and at Mr. Wraxall's mercy; and that inquirer was not inclined to spare him.

'Herr Nielsen,' he said, 'I have found out something about the Black Pilgrimage. You may as well tell me what you know. What did the Count bring back with him?'

Swedes are habitually slow, perhaps, in answering, or perhaps the landlord was an exception. I am not sure; but Mr. Wraxall notes that the landlord spent at least one minute in looking at him before he said anything at all. Then he came up to his guest, and with a good deal of effort he spoke:

'Mr. Wraxall, I can tell you this one little tale, and no more – not any more. You must not ask anything when I have done. In my grandfather's time – that is, ninety-two years ago – there were two men who said: "The Count is dead; we do not care for him. We will go tonight and have a free hunt in his wood" – the long wood on the hill that you have seen behind Råbäck. Well, those that heard them say this, they said: "No, do not go; we are sure you will meet with persons walking who should not be walking. They should be resting, not walking." These men laughed. There were no forest-men to keep the wood, because no one wished to hunt there. The family were not here at the house. These men could do what they wished.

'Very well, they go to the wood that night. My grandfather was sitting here in this room. It was the summer, and a light night. With the window open, he could see out to the wood, and hear.

'So he sat there, and two or three men with him, and they listened. At first they hear nothing at all; then they hear someone – you know how far away it is – they hear someone scream, just as if the most inside part of his soul was twisted out of him. All of them in the room caught hold of each other, and they sat so for three-quarters of an hour. Then they hear someone else, only about three hundred ells off. They hear him laugh out loud: it was not one of those two men that laughed, and, indeed, they have all of them said that it was not any man at all. After that they hear a great door shut.

'Then, when it was just light with the sun, they all went to the priest. They said to him:

' "Father, put on your gown and your ruff, and come to bury these men, Anders Bjornsen and Hans Thorbjorn."

'You understand that they were sure these men were dead. So they went to the wood – my grandfather never forgot this. He said they were all like so many dead men themselves. The priest, too, he was in a white fear. He said when they came to him:

' "I heard one cry in the night, and I heard one laugh afterwards. If I cannot forget that, I shall not be able to sleep again."

'So they went to the wood, and they found these men on the edge of the wood. Hans Thorbjorn was standing with his back against a tree, and all the time he was pushing with his hands – pushing something away from him which was not there. So he was not dead. And they led him away, and took him to the house at Nykjoping, and he died before the winter; but he went on pushing with his hands. Also Anders Bjornsen was there; but he was dead. And I tell you this about Anders Bjornsen, that he was once a beautiful man, but now his face was not there, because the flesh of it was sucked away off the bones. You understand that? My grandfather did not forget that. And they laid him on the bier which they brought, and they put a cloth over his head, and the priest walked before; and they began to sing the psalm for the dead as well as they could. So, as they were singing the end of the first verse, one fell down, who was carrying the head of the bier, and the others looked back, and they saw that the cloth had fallen off, and the eyes of Anders Bjornsen were looking up, because there was nothing to close over them. And this they could not bear. Therefore the priest laid the cloth upon him, and sent for a spade, and they buried him in that place.'

The next day Mr. Wraxall records that the deacon called

for him soon after his breakfast, and took him to the church and mausoleum. He noticed that the key of the latter was hung on a nail just by the pulpit, and it occurred to him that, as the church door seemed to be left unlocked as a rule, it would not be difficult for him to pay a second and more private visit to the monuments if there proved to be more of interest among them than could be digested at first. The building, when he entered it, he found not unimposing. The monuments, mostly large erections of the seventeenth and eighteenth centuries, were dignified if luxuriant, and the epitaphs and heraldry were copious. The central space of the domed room was occupied by three copper sarcophagi, covered with finely-engraved ornament. Two of them had as is commonly the case in Denmark and Sweden, a large metal crucifix on the lid. The third, that of Count Magnus, as it appeared, had, instead of that, a full-length effigy engraved upon it, and round the edge were several bands of similar ornament representing various scenes. One was a battle, with cannon belching out smoke, and walled towns, and troops of pikemen. Another showed an execution. In a third, among trees, was a man running at full speed, with flying hair and outstretched hands. After him followed a strange form; it would be hard to say whether the artist had intended it for a man, and was unable to give the requisite similitude; or whether it was intentionally made as monstrous as it looked. In view of the skill with which the rest of the drawing was done, Mr. Wraxall felt inclined to adopt the latter idea. The figure was unduly short, and was for the most part muffled in a hooded garment which swept the ground. The only part of the form which projected from that shelter was not shaped like any hand or arm. Mr. Wraxall compares it to the tentacle of a devil-fish, and continues: 'On seeing this, I said to myself, "This, then, which is evidently an allegorical representation of some kind – a fiend pursuing a hunted soul – may be the origin of the story of Count Magnus and his mysterious companion. Let us see how the huntsman is pictured: doubtless it will be a demon blowing his horn." ' But, as it turned out, there was no such sensational figure, only the semblance of a cloaked man on a hillock, who stood leaning on a stick, and watching the hunt with an interest which the engraver had tried to express in his attitude.

Mr. Wraxall noted the finely-worked and massive steel padlocks – three in number – which secured the sarcophagus. One of them, he saw, was detached, and lay on the pavement. And then, unwilling to delay the deacon longer or to waste his own working-time, he made his way onward to the manor house.

'It is curious,' he notes, 'how on retracing a familiar path one's thoughts engross one to the absolute exclusion of surrounding objects. Tonight, for the second time, I had entirely failed to notice where I was going (I had planned a private visit to the tomb-house to copy the epitaphs), when I suddenly, as it were, awoke to consciousness, and found myself (as before) turning in at the churchyard gate, and, I believe, singing or chanting some such words as, "Are you awake, Count Magnus? Are you asleep, Count Magnus?" and then something more which I have failed to recollect. It seemed to me that I must have been behaving in this nonsensical way for some time.'

He found the key of the mausoleum where he had expected to find it, and copied the greater part of what he wanted; in fact, he stayed until the light began to fail him.

'I must have been wrong,' he writes, 'in saying that one of the padlocks of my Count's sarcophagus was unfastened; I see tonight that two are loose. I picked both up, and laid them carefully on the window-ledge, after trying unsuccessfully to close them. The remaining one is still firm, and, though I take it to be a spring lock, I cannot guess how it is opened. Had I succeeded in undoing it, I am almost afraid I should have taken the liberty of opening the sarcophagus. It is strange, the interest I feel in the personality of this, I fear, somewhat ferocious and grim old noble.'

The day following was, as it turned out, the last of Mr. Wraxall's stay at Råbäck. He received letters connected with certain investments which made it desirable that he should return to England; his work among the papers was practically done, and travelling was slow. He decided, therefore, to make his farewells, put some finishing touches to his notes, and be off.

These finishing touches and farewells, as it turned out, took more time than he had expected. The hospitable family insisted on his staying to dine with them – they dined at three – and it was verging on half past six before he was outside the iron gates of Råbäck. He dwelt on every step of his walk by the lake, determined to saturate himself, now that he trod it for the last time, in the sentiment of the place and hour. And when he reached the summit of the churchyard knoll, he lingered for many minutes, gazing at the limitless prospect of wood near and distant, all dark beneath a sky of liquid green. When at last he turned to go, the thought struck him that surely he must bid farewell to Count Magnus as well as the rest of the De la Gardies. The church was but twenty yards away, and he knew where the key of the mausoleum hung. It was not long before he was standing over the great copper coffin, and, as usual, talking to himself aloud. 'You may have been a bit of a rascal in your time, Magnus,' he was saying, 'but for all that I should like to see you, or, rather—'

'Just at that instant,' he says, 'I felt a blow on my foot. Hastily enough I drew it back, and something fell on the pavement with a clash. It was the third, the last of the three padlocks which had fastened the sarcophagus. I stooped to pick it up, and – Heaven is my witness that I am writing only the bare truth – before I raised myself there was a sound of metal hinges creaking, and I distinctly saw the lid shifting upwards. I may have behaved like a coward, but I could not for my life stay for one moment. I was outside that dreadful building in less time than I can write – almost as quickly as I could have said – the words; and what frightens me yet more, I could not turn the key in the lock. As I sit here in my room noting these facts, I ask myself (it was not twenty minutes ago) whether that noise of creaking metal continued, and I cannot tell whether it did or not. I only know that there was something more than I have written that alarmed me, but whether it was sound or sight I am not able to remember. What is this that I have done?'

Poor Mr. Wraxall! He set out on his journey to England on the next day, as he had planned, and he reached England in safety; and yet, as I gather from his changed hand and inconsequent jottings, a broken man. One of several small notebooks that have come to me with his papers gives, not a key to, but a kind of inkling of, his experiences. Much of his journey was made by canal-boat, and I find not less than six painful attempts to enumerate and describe his fellow-passengers. The entries are of this kind:

'24. Pastor of village in Skåne. Usual black coat and soft black hat.
'25. Commercial traveller from Stockholm going to Trollhättan. Black cloak, brown hat.
'26. Man in long black cloak, broad-leafed hat, very old-fashioned.'

This entry is lined out, and a note added: 'Perhaps identical with No. 13. Have not yet seen his face.' On referring to No. 13, I find that he is a Roman priest in a cassock.

The net result of the reckoning is always the same. Twenty-eight people appear in the enumeration, one being always a man in a long black cloak and broad hat, and the other a 'short figure in dark cloak and hood'. On the other hand, it is always noted that only twenty-six passengers appear at meals, and that the man in the cloak is perhaps absent, and the short figure is certainly absent.

On reaching England, it appears that Mr. Wraxall landed at Harwich, and that he resolved at once to put himself out of the reach of some person or persons whom he never specifies, but whom he had evidently come to regard as his pursuers. Accordingly he took a vehicle – it was a closed fly – not trusting the railway, and drove across country to the village of Belchamp St. Paul. It was about nine o'clock on a moonlight August night when he neared the place. He was sitting forward, and looking out of the window at the fields and thickets – there was little else to be seen – racing past him. Suddenly he came to a cross-road. At the corner two figures were standing motionless; both were in dark cloaks; the taller one wore a hat, the shorter a hood. He had no time to see their faces, nor did they make any motion that he could discern. Yet the horse shied violently and broke into a gallop, and Mr. Wraxall sank back into his seat in something like desperation. He had seen them before.

Arrived at Belchamp St. Paul, he was fortunate enough to find a decent furnished lodging, and for the next twenty-four hours he lived, comparatively speaking, in peace. His last notes were written on this day. They are too disjointed and ejaculatory to be given here in full, but the substance of them is clear enough. He is expecting a visit from his pursuers – how or when he knows not – and his constant cry is 'What has he done?' and 'Is there no hope?' Doctors, he knows, would call him mad, policemen would laugh at him. The parson is away. What can he do but lock his door and cry to God?

People still remembered last year at Belchamp St. Paul how a strange gentleman came one evening in August years back; and how the next morning but one he was found dead, and there was an inquest; and the jury that viewed the body fainted, seven of 'em did, and none of 'em wouldn't speak to what they see, and the verdict was visitation of God; and how the people as kep' the 'ouse moved out that same week, and went away from that part. But they do not, I think, know that any glimmer of light has ever been thrown, or could be thrown, on the mystery. It so happened that last year the little house came into my hands as part of a legacy.

It had stood empty since 1863, and there seemed no prospect of letting it; so I had it pulled down, and the papers of which I have given you an abstract were found in a forgotten cupboard under the window in the best bedroom.

Lost Hearts

It was, as far as I can ascertain, in September of the year 1811 that a post-chaise drew up before the door of Aswarby Hall, in the heart of Lincolnshire. The little boy who was the only passenger in the chaise, and who jumped out as soon as it had stopped, looked about him with the keenest curiosity during the short interval that elapsed between the ringing of the bell and the opening of the hall door. He saw a tall, square, red-brick house, built in the reign of Anne; a stone-pillared porch had been added in the purer classical style of 1790; the windows of the house were many, tall and narrow, with small panes and thick white woodwork. A pediment, pierced with a round window, crowned the front. There were wings to right and left, connected by curious glazed galleries, supported by colonnades, with the central block. These wings plainly contained the stables and offices of the house. Each was surmounted by an ornamental cupola with a gilded vane.

An evening light shone on the building, making the window-panes glow like so many fires. Away from the Hall in front stretched a flat park studded with oaks and fringed with firs, which stood out against the sky. The clock in the church-tower, buried in trees on the edge of the park, only its golden weather-cock catching the light, was striking six, and the sound came gently beating down the wind. It was altogether a pleasant impression, though tinged with the sort of melancholy appropriate to an evening in early autumn, that was conveyed to the mind of the boy who was standing in the porch waiting for the door to open to him.

The post-chaise had brought him from Warwickshire, where, some six months before, he had been left an orphan. Now, owing to the generous offer of his elderly cousin, Mr Abney, he had come to live at Aswarby. The offer was unexpected, because all who knew anything of Mr Abney looked upon him as a somewhat austere recluse, into whose steady-going household the advent of a small boy would import a new and, it seemed, incongruous element. The truth is that very little was known of Mr Abney's pursuits or temper. The

Professor of Greek at Cambridge had been heard to say that no one knew more of the religious beliefs of the later pagans than did the owner of Aswarby. Certainly his library con-tained all the then available books bearing on the Mysteries, the Orphic poems, the worship of Mithras, and the Neo-Platonists. In the marble-paved hall stood a fine group of Mithras slaying a bull, which had been imported from the Levant at great expense by the owner. He had contributed a description of it to the *Gentleman's Magazine*, and he had written a remarkable series of articles in the *Critical Museum* on the superstitions of the Romans of the Lower Empire. He was looked upon, in fine, as a man wrapped up in his books, and it was a matter of great surprise among his neighbours that he could even have heard of his orphan cousin, Stephen Elliott, much more that he should have volunteered to make him an inmate of Aswarby Hall.

Whatever may have been expected by his neighbours, it is certain that Mr Abney – the tall, the thin, the austere – seemed inclined to give his young cousin a kindly reception. The moment the front door was opened he darted out of his study, rubbing his hands with delight.

'How are you, my boy? – how are you? How old are you?' said he – 'that is, you are not too much tired, I hope, by your journey to eat your supper?'

'No, thank you, sir,' said Master Elliott; 'I am pretty well.'

'That's a good lad,' said Mr Abney. 'And how old are you, my boy?'

It seemed a little odd that he should have asked the question twice in the first two minutes of their acquaintance.

'I'm twelve years old next birthday, sir,' said Stephen.

'And when is your birthday, my dear boy? Eleventh of September, eh? That's well – that's very well. Nearly a year hence, isn't it? I like – ha, ha! – I like to get these things down in my book. Sure it's twelve? Certain?'

'Yes, quite sure, sir.'

'Well, well! Take him to Mrs Bunch's room, Parkes, and let him have his tea – supper – whatever it is.'

'Yes, sir,' answered the staid Mr Parkes; and conducted Stephen to the lower regions.

Mrs Bunch was the most comfortable and human person whom Stephen had as yet met in Aswarby. She made him completely at home; they were great friends in a quarter of an hour: and great friends they remained. Mrs Bunch had been born in the neighbourhood some fifty-five years before the date of Stephen's arrival, and her residence at the Hall was of twenty years' standing. Consequently, if anyone knew the ins and outs of the house and the district, Mrs Bunch knew them; and she was by no means disinclined to communicate her information.

Certainly there were plenty of things about the Hall and the Hall gardens which Stephen, who was of an adventurous and inquiring turn, was anxious to have explained to him. 'Who built the temple at the end of the laurel walk? Who was the old man whose picture hung on the staircase, sitting at a table, with a skull under his hand?' These and many similar points were cleared up by the resources of Mrs Bunch's powerful intellect. There were others, however, of which the explanations furnished were less satisfactory.

One November evening Stephen was sitting by the fire in the housekeeper's room reflecting on his surroundings.

'Is Mr Abney a good man, and will he go to heaven?' he suddenly asked, with the peculiar confidence which children possess in the ability of their elders to settle these questions, the decision of which is believed to be reserved for other tribunals.

'Good? – bless the child!' said Mrs Bunch. 'Master's as kind a soul as ever I see! Didn't I never tell you of the little boy as he took in out of the street, as you may say, this seven years back? and the little girl, two years after I first come here?'

'No. Do tell me all about them, Mrs Bunch – now this minute!'

'Well,' said Mrs Bunch, 'the little girl I don't seem to

recollect so much about. I know master brought her back with him from his walk one day, and give orders to Mrs Ellis, as was housekeeper then, as she should be took every care with. And the pore child hadn't no one belonging to her – she telled me so her own self – and here she lived with us a matter of three weeks it might be; and then, whether she were something of a gipsy in her blood or what not, but one morning she out of her bed afore any of us had opened an eye, and neither track nor yet trace of her have I set eyes on since. Master was wonderful put about, and had all the ponds dragged; but it's my belief she was had away by them gipsies, for there was singing round the house for as much as an hour the night she went, and Parkes, he declare as he heard them a-calling in the woods all that afternoon. Dear, dear! a hodd child she was, so silent in her ways and all, but I was wonderful taken up with her, so domesticated she was – surprising.'

'And what about the little boy?' said Stephen.

'Ah, that pore boy!' sighed Mrs Bunch. 'He were a foreigner – Jevanny he called hisself – and he come a-tweaking his 'urdy-gurdy round and about the drive one winter day, and master 'ad him in that minute, and ast all about where he came from, and how old he was, and how he made his way, and where was his relatives, and all as kind as heart could wish. But it went the same way with him. They're a hunruly lot, them foreign nations, I do suppose, and he was off one fine morning just the same as the girl. Why he went and what he done was our question for as much as a year after; for he never took his 'urdy-gurdy, and there it lays on the shelf.'

The remainder of the evening was spent by Stephen in miscellaneous cross-examination of Mrs Bunch and in efforts to extract a tune from the hurdy-gurdy.

That night he had a curious dream. At the end of the passage at the top of the house, in which his bedroom was situated, there was an old disused bathroom. It was kept locked, but the upper half of the door was glazed, and, since the muslin curtains which used to hang there had long been gone, you could look in and see the lead-lined bath affixed to the wall on the right hand, with its head towards the window.

On the night of which I am speaking, Stephen Elliott found himself, as he thought, looking through the glazed door. The moon was shining through the window, and he was gazing at a figure which lay in the bath.

His description of what he saw reminds me of what I once beheld myself in the famous vaults of St Michan's Church in Dublin, which possess the horrid property of preserving corpses from decay for centuries. A figure inexpressibly thin and pathetic, of a dusty leaden colour, enveloped in a shroud-like garment, the thin lips crooked into a faint and dreadful smile, the hands pressed tightly over the region of the heart.

As he looked upon it, a distant, almost inaudible moan seemed to issue from its lips, and the arms began to stir. The terror of the sight forced Stephen backwards, and he awoke to the fact that he was indeed standing on the cold boarded floor of the passage in the full light of the moon. With a courage which I do not think can be common among boys of his age, he went to the door of the bathroom to ascertain if the figure of his dream were really there. It was not, and he went back to bed.

Mrs Bunch was much impressed next morning by his story, and went so far as to replace the muslin curtain over the glazed door of the bathroom. Mr Abney, moreover, to whom he confided his experiences at breakfast, was greatly interested, and made notes of the matter in what he called 'his book'.

The spring equinox was approaching, as Mr Abney frequently reminded his cousin, adding that this had been always considered by the ancients to be a critical time for the young: that Stephen would do well to take care of himself, and to shut his bedroom window at night; and that Censorinus had some valuable remarks on the subject. Two incidents that occurred about this time made an impression upon Stephen's mind.

The first was after an unusually uneasy and oppressed night

that he had passed – though he could not recall any particular dream that he had had.

The following evening Mrs Bunch was occupying herself in mending his nightgown.

'Gracious me, Master Stephen!' she broke forth rather irritably, 'how do you manage to tear your nightdress all to flinders this way? Look here, sir, what trouble you do give to poor servants that have to darn and mend after you!'

There was indeed a most destructive and apparently wanton series of slits or scorings in the garment, which would undoubtedly require a skilful needle to make good. They were confined to the left side of the chest – long, parallel slits, about six inches in length, some of them not quite piercing the texture of the linen. Stephen could only express his entire ignorance of their origin: he was sure they were not there the night before.

'But,' he said, 'Mrs Bunch, they are just the same as the scratches on the outside of my bedroom door; and I'm sure I never had anything to do with making *them*.'

Mrs Bunch gazed at him open-mouthed, then snatched up a candle, departed hastily from the room, and was heard making her way upstairs. In a few minutes she came down.

'Well,' she said, 'Master Stephen, it's a funny thing to me how them marks and scratches can 'a' come there – too high up for any cat or dog to 'ave made 'em, much less a rat: for all the world like a Chinaman's finger-nails, as my uncle in the tea-trade used to tell us of when we was girls together. I wouldn't say nothing to master, not if I was you, Master Stephen, my dear; and just turn the key of the door when you go to your bed.'

'I always do, Mrs Bunch, as soon as I've said my prayers.'

'Ah, that's a good child: always say your prayers, and then no one can't hurt you.'

Herewith Mrs Bunch addressed herself to mending the injured nightgown, with intervals of meditation, until bedtime. This was on a Friday night in March, 1812.

On the following evening the usual duet of Stephen and Mrs Bunch was augmented by the sudden arrival of Mr Parkes, the butler, who as a rule kept himself rather *to* himself in his own pantry. He did not see that Stephen was there: he was, moreover, flustered, and less slow of speech than was his wont.

'Master may get up his own wine, if he likes, of an evening,' was his first remark. 'Either I do it in the daytime or not at all, Mrs Bunch. I don't know what it may be: very like it's the rats, or the wind got into the cellars; but I'm not so young as I was, and I can't go through with it as I have done.'

'Well, Mr Parkes, you know it is a surprising place for the rats, is the Hall.'

'I'm not denying that, Mrs Bunch; and, to be sure, many a time I've heard the tale from the men in the shipyards about the rat that could speak. I never laid no confidence in that before; but tonight, if I'd demeaned myself to lay my ear to the door of the further bin, I could pretty much have heard what they was saying.'

'Oh, there, Mr Parkes, I've no patience with your fancies! Rats talking in the wine-cellar indeed!'

'Well, Mrs Bunch, I've no wish to argue with you: all I say is, if you choose to go to the far bin, and lay your ear to the door, you may prove my words this minute.'

'What nonsense you do talk, Mr Parkes – not fit for children to listen to! Why, you'll be frightening Master Stephen there out of his wits.'

'What! Master Stephen?' said Parkes, awaking to the consciousness of the boy's presence. 'Master Stephen knows well enough when I'm a-playing a joke with you, Mrs Bunch.'

In fact, Master Stephen knew much too well to suppose that Parkes had in the first instance intended a joke. He was interested, not altogether pleasantly, in the situation; but all his questions were unsuccessful in inducing the butler to give any more detailed account of his experiences in the wine-cellar.

*

We have now arrived at 24th March, 1812. It was a day of curious experiences for Stephen: a windy, noisy day, which filled the house and the gardens with a restless impression. As Stephen stood by the fence of the grounds, and looked out into the park, he felt as if an endless procession of unseen people were sweeping past him on the wind, borne on restlessly and aimlessly, vainly striving to stop themselves, to catch at something that might arrest their flight and bring them once again into contact with the living world of which they had formed a part. After luncheon that day Mr Abney said:

'Stephen, my boy, do you think you could manage to come to me tonight as late as eleven o'clock in my study? I shall be busy until that time, and I wish to show you something connected with your future life which it is most important that you should know. You are not to mention this matter to Mrs Bunch nor to anyone else in the house; and you had better go to your room at the usual time.'

Here was a new excitement added to life: Stephen eagerly grasped at the opportunity of sitting up till eleven o'clock. He looked in at the library door on his way upstairs that evening, and saw a brazier, which he had often noticed in the corner of the room, moved out before the fire; an old silver-gilt cup stood on the table, filled with red wine, and some written sheets of paper lay near it. Mr Abney was sprinkling some incense on the brazier from a round silver box as Stephen passed, but did not seem to notice his step.

The wind had fallen, and there was a still night and a full moon. At about ten o'clock Stephen was standing at the open window of his bedroom, looking out over the country. Still as the night was, the mysterious population of the distant moonlit woods was not yet lulled to rest. From time to time strange cries as of lost and despairing wanderers sounded from across the mere. They might be the notes of owls or waterbirds, yet they did not quite resemble either sound. Were not they coming nearer? Now they sounded from the nearer side of the water, and in a few moments they seemed to be floating about among the shrubberies. Then they ceased; but just as Stephen was thinking of shutting the window and resuming his reading of *Robinson Crusoe*, he caught sight of two figures standing on the gravelled terrace that ran along the garden side of the Hall – the figures of a boy and girl, as it seemed; they stood side by side, looking up at the windows. Something in the form of the girl recalled irresistibly his dream of the figure in the bath. The boy inspired him with more acute fear.

Whilst the girl stood still, half smiling, with her hands clasped over her heart, the boy, a thin shape, with black hair and ragged clothing, raised his arms in the air with an appearance of menace and of unappeasable hunger and longing. The moon shone upon his almost transparent hands, and Stephen saw that the nails were fearfully long and that the light shone through them. As he stood with his arms thus raised, he disclosed a terrifying spectacle. On the left side of his chest there opened a black and gaping rent; and there fell upon Stephen's brain, rather than upon his ear, the impression of one of those hungry and desolate cries that he had heard resounding over the woods of Aswarby all that evening. In another moment this dreadful pair had moved swiftly and noiselessly over the dry gravel, and he saw them no more.

Inexpressibly frightened as he was, he determined to take his candle and go down to Mr Abney's study, for the hour appointed for their meeting was near at hand. The study or library opened out of the front hall on one side, and Stephen, urged on by his terrors, did not take long in getting there. To effect an entrance was not so easy. The door was not locked, he felt sure, for the key was on the outside of it as usual. His repeated knocks produced no answer. Mr Abney was engaged: he was speaking. What! why did he try to cry out? and why was the cry choked in his throat? Had he, too, seen the mysterious children? But now everything was quiet, and the door yielded to Stephen's terrified and frantic pushing.

✻

On the table in Mr Abney's study certain papers were found which explained the situation to Stephen Elliott when he was of an age to understand them. The most important sentences were as follows:

'It was a belief very strongly and generally held by the ancients – of whose wisdom in these matters I have had such experience as induces me to place confidence in their asser-tions – that by enacting certain processes which to us moderns have something of a barbaric complexion, a very remarkable enlightenment of the spiritual faculties in man may be attained: that, for example, by absorbing the personalities of a certain number of his fellow-creatures, an individual may gain a complete ascendancy over those orders of spiritual beings which control the elemental forces of our universe.

'It is recorded of Simon Magus that he was able to fly in the air, to become invisible, or to assume any form he pleased, by the agency of the soul of a boy whom, to use the libellous phrase employed by the author of the *Clementine Recognitions*, he had 'murdered'. I find it set down, moreover, with con-siderable detail in the writings of Hermes Trismegistus, that similar happy results may be produced by the absorption of the hearts of not less than three human beings below the age of twenty-one years. To the testing of the truth of this receipt I have devoted the greater part of the last twenty years, selecting as the *corpora vilia* of my experiment such persons as could conveniently be removed without occasioning a sen-sible gap in society. The first step I effected by the removal of one Phoebe Stanley, a girl of gipsy extraction, on 24th March, 1792. The second, by the removal of a wandering Italian lad, named Giovanni Paoli, on the night of 23rd March, 1805. The final 'victim' – to employ a word repugnant in the highest degree to my feelings – must be my cousin, Stephen Elliott. His day must be this 24th March, 1812.

'The best means of effecting the required absorption is to remove the heart from the *living* subject, to reduce it to ashes, and to mingle them with about a pint of some red wine, preferably port. The remains of the first two subjects, at least, it will be well to conceal: a disused bathroom or wine-cellar will be found convenient for such a purpose. Some annoyance may be experienced from the psychic portion of the subjects, which popular language dignifies with the name of ghosts. But the man of philosophic temperament – to whom alone the experiment is appropriate – will be little prone to attach importance to the feeble efforts of these beings to wreak their vengeance on him. I contemplate with the liveliest satisfaction the enlarged and emancipated existence which the experiment, if successful, will confer on me; not only placing me beyond the reach of human justice (so-called), but eliminating to a great extent the prospect of death itself.'

*

Mr Abney was found in his chair, his head thrown back, his face stamped with an expression of rage, fright, and mortal pain. In his left side was a terrible lacerated wound, exposing the heart. There was no blood on his hands, and a long knife that lay on the table was perfectly clean. A savage wild-cat might have inflicted the injuries. The window of the study was open, and it was the opinion of the coroner that Mr Abney had met his death by the agency of some wild creature. But Stephen Elliott's study of the papers I have quoted led him to a very different conclusion.

Martin's Close

Some few years back I was staying with the rector of a parish in the West, where the society to which I belong owns property. I was to go over some of this land: and, on the first morning of my visit, soon after breakfast, the estate carpenter and general handy-man, John Hill, was announced as in readiness to accompany us. The rector asked which part of the parish we were to visit that morning. The estate map was produced, and when we had showed him our round, he put his finger on a particular spot. 'Don't forget,' he said, 'to ask John Hill about Martin's Close when you get there. I should like to hear what he tells you.' 'What ought he to tell us?' I said. 'I haven't the slightest idea,' said the rector, 'or, if that is not exactly true, it will do till lunch-time.' And here he was called away.

We set out; John Hill is not a man to withhold such information as he possesses on any point, and you may gather from him much that is of interest about the people of the place and their talk. An unfamiliar word, or one that he thinks ought to be unfamiliar to you, he will usually spell – as c-o-b cob, and the like. It is not, however, relevant to my purpose to record his conversation before the moment when we reached Martin's Close. The bit of land is noticeable, for it is one of the smallest enclosures you are likely to see – a very few square yards, hedged in with quickset on all sides, and without any gate or gap leading into it. You might take it for a small cottage garden long deserted, but that it lies away from the village and bears no trace of cultivation. It is at no great distance from the road, and is part of what is there called a moor, in other words, a rough upland pasture cut up into largish fields.

'Why is this little bit hedged off so?' I asked, and John Hill (whose answer I cannot represent as perfectly as I should like) was not at fault. 'That's what we call Martin's Close, sir: 'tes a curious thing 'bout that bit of land, sir: goes by the name of Martin's Close, sir. M-a-r-t-i-n Martin. Beg pardon, sir, did Rector tell you to make inquiry of me 'bout that, sir?' 'Yes, he did.' 'Ah, I thought so much, sir. I was tell'n Rector 'bout that last week, and he was very much interested. It 'pears there's a murderer buried there, sir, by the name of Martin. Old Mr. Samuel Saunders, that formerly lived yurr at what we call South-town, sir, he had a long tale 'bout that, sir: terrible murder done 'pon a young woman, sir. Cut her throat and cast her in the water down yurr.' 'Was he hung for it?' 'Yes, sir, he was hung just up yurr on the roadway, by what I've 'eard, on the Holy Innocents' Day, many 'undred years ago, by the man that went by the name of the bloody judge: terrible red and bloody, I've 'eard.' 'Was his name Jefferies, do you think?' 'Might be possible 'twas – Jefferies – J-e-f – Jefferies. I reckon 'twas, and the tale I've 'eard many times from Mr. Saunders, – how this young man Martin – George Martin – was troubled before his crule action come to light by the young woman's sperit.' 'How was that, do you know?' 'No, sir, I don't exactly know how 'twas with it: but by what I've 'eard he was fairly tormented: and rightly tu. Old Mr. Saunders, he told a history regarding a cupboard down yurr in the New Inn. According to what he related, this young woman's sperit come out of this cupboard: but I don't racollact the matter.'

This was the sum of John Hill's information. We passed on, and in due time I reported what I had heard to the Rector. He was able to show me from the parish account-books that a gibbet had been paid for in 1684, and a grave dug in the following year, both for the benefit of George Martin; but he was unable to suggest any one in the parish, Saunders being now gone, who was likely to throw any further light on the story.

Naturally, upon my return to the neighbourhood of libraries, I made search in the more obvious places. The trial seemed to be nowhere reported. A newspaper of the time, and one or more newsletters, however, had some short notices, from which I learnt that, on the ground of local prejudice against the prisoner (he was described as a young gentleman of a good estate), the venue had been moved from Exeter to London; that Jefferies had been the judge, and death the sentence, and that there had been some 'singular passages' in the evidence. Nothing further transpired till September of this year. A friend who knew me to be interested in Jefferies then sent me a leaf torn out of a secondhand bookseller's catalogue with the entry: JEFFERIES, JUDGE: *Interesting old MS. trial for murder*, and so forth, from which I gathered, to my delight, that I could become possessed, for a very few shillings, of what seemed to be a verbatim report, in shorthand, of the Martin trial. I telegraphed for the manuscript and got it. It was a thin bound volume, provided with a title written in longhand by some one in the eighteenth century, who had also added this note: 'My father, who took these notes in court, told me that the prisoner's friends had made interest with Judge Jefferies that no report should be put out: he had intended doing this himself when times were better, and had shew'd it to the Revd. Mr. Glanvil, who incourag'd his design very warmly, but death surpriz'd them both before it could be brought to an accomplishment.'

The initials W. G. are appended; I am advised that the original reporter may have been T. Gurney, who appears in that capacity in more than one State trial.

This was all that I could read for myself. After no long delay I heard of some one who was capable of deciphering the shorthand of the seventeenth century, and a little time ago the type-written copy of the whole manuscript was laid before me. The portions which I shall communicate here help to fill in the very imperfect outline which subsists in the memories of John Hill and, I suppose, one or two others who live on the scene of the events.

The report begins with a species of preface, the general effect of which is that the copy is not that actually taken in court, though it is a true copy in regard of the notes of what was said; but that the writer has added to it some 'remarkable passages' that took place during the trial, and has made this present fair copy of the whole, intending at some favourable time to publish it; but has not put it into longhand, lest it should fall into the possession of unauthorised persons, and he or his family be deprived of the profit. The report then begins:—

This case came on to be tried on Wednesday, the 19th of November, between our sovereign lord the King, and George Martin Esquire, of (I take leave to omit some of the place-names), at a sessions of oyer and terminer and gaol delivery, at the Old Bailey, and the prisoner, being in Newgate, was brought to the bar.

Clerk of the Crown. George Martin, hold up thy hand (which he did).

Then the indictment was read, which set forth that the prisoner 'not having the fear of God before his eyes, but being moved and seduced by the instigation of the devil, upon the 15th day of May, in the 36th year of our sovereign lord King Charles the Second, with force and arms in the parish aforesaid, in and upon Ann Clark, spinster, of the same place, in the peace of God and of our said sovereign lord the King then and there being, feloniously, wilfully, and of your malice afore-thought did make an assault and with a certain knife value a penny the throat of the said Ann Clark then and there did cut, of the which wound the said Ann Clark then and there did die, and the body of the said Ann Clark did cast into a certain pond of water situate in the same parish (with more that is not material to our purpose) against the peace of our sovereign lord the King, his crown and dignity.'

Then the prisoner prayed a copy of the indictment.

L.C.J (Sir George Jefferies). What is this? Sure you know that is never allowed. Besides, here is a plain indictment as ever I heard; you have nothing to do but to plead to it.

Pris. My lord, I apprehend there may be matter of law arising out of the indictment, and I would humbly beg the court to assign me to counsel to consider of it. Besides, my lord, I believe it was done in another case: copy of the indictment was allowed.

L.C.J. What case was that?

Pris. Truly, my lord, I have been kept close prisoner ever since I came up from Exeter Castle, and no one allowed to come at me and no one to advise with.

L.C.J. But I say, what was that case you allege?

Pris. My lord, I cannot tell your lordship precisely the name of the case, but it is in my mind that there was such an one, and I would humbly desire—

L.C.J. All this is nothing. Name your case, and we will tell you whether there be any matter for you in it. God forbid but you should have anything that may be allowed you by law: but this is against law, and we must keep the course of the court.

Att. Gen. (Sir Robert Sawyer). My lord, we pray for the King that he may be asked to plead.

Cl. of Ct. Are you guilty of the murder whereof you stand indicted, or not guilty?

Pris. My lord, I would humbly offer this to the court. If I plead now, shall I have an opportunity after to except against the indictment?

L.C.J. Yes, yes, that comes after verdict: that will be saved to you, and counsel assigned if there be matter of law: but that which you have now to do is to plead.

Then after some little parleying with the court (which seemed strange upon such a plain indictment) the prisoner pleaded *Not Guilty.*

Cl. of Ct. Culprit. How wilt thou be tried?

Pris. By God and my country.

Cl. of Ct. God send thee a good deliverance.

L.C.J. Why, how is this? Here has been a great to-do that you should not be tried at Exeter by your country, but be brought here to London, and now you ask to be tried by your country. Must we send you to Exeter again?

Pris. My lord, I understood it was the form.

L.C.J. So it is, man: we spoke only in the way of pleasantness. Well, go on and swear the jury.

So they were sworn. I omit the names. There was no challenging on the prisoner's part, for, as he said, he did not know any of the persons called. Thereupon the prisoner asked for the use of pen, ink, and paper, to which the L.C.J. replied: 'Ay, ay, in God's name let him have it.' Then the usual charge was delivered to the jury, and the case opened by the junior counsel for the King, Mr. Dolben.

The Attorney-General followed:—

May it please your lordship, and you gentlemen of the jury, I am of counsel for the King against the prisoner at the bar. You have heard that he stands indicted for a murder done upon the person of a young girl. Such crimes as this you may perhaps reckon not to be uncommon, and, indeed, in these times, I am sorry to say it, there is scarce any fact so barbarous and unnatural but what we may hear almost daily instances of it. But I must confess that in this murder that is charged upon the prisoner there are some particular features that mark it out to be such as I hope has but seldom if ever been perpetrated upon English ground. For as we shall make it appear, the person murdered was a poor country girl (whereas the prisoner is a gentleman of a proper estate) and, besides that, was one to whom Providence had not given the full use of her intellects, but was what is termed among us commonly an innocent or natural: such an one, therefore, as one would have supposed a gentleman of the prisoner's quality more likely to overlook, or, if he did notice her, to be moved to compassion for her unhappy condition, than to lift up his hand against her in the very horrid and barbarous manner which we shall show you he used.

Now to begin at the beginning and open the matter to you orderly: About Christmas of last year, that is the year 1683, this gentleman, Mr. Martin, having newly come back into his own country from the University of Cambridge, some of his neighbours, to show him what civility they could (for his family is one that stands in very good repute all over that country) entertained him here and there at their Christmas merrymakings, so that he was constantly riding to and fro, from one house to another, and sometimes, when the place of his destination was distant, or for other reason, as the unsafeness of the roads, he would be constrained to lie the night at an inn. In this way it happened that he came, a day or two after the Christmas, to the place where this young girl lived with her parents, and put up at the inn there, called the New Inn, which is, as I am informed, a house of good repute. Here was some dancing going on among the people of the place, and Ann Clark had been brought in, it seems, by her elder sister to look on; but being, as I have said, of weak understanding, and, besides that, very uncomely in her appearance, it was not likely she should take much part in the merriment; and accordingly was but standing by in a corner of the room. The prisoner at the bar, seeing her, one must suppose by way of a jest, asked her would she dance with him. And in spite of what her sister and others could say to prevent it and to dissuade her—

L.C.J. Come, Mr. Attorney, we are not set here to listen to tales of Christmas parties in taverns. I would not interrupt you, but sure you have more weighty matters than this. You will be telling us next what tune they danced to.

Att. My lord, I would not take up the time of the court with what is not material: but we reckon it to be material to show how this unlikely acquaintance begun: and as for the tune, I believe, indeed, our evidence will show that even that hath a bearing on the matter in hand.

L.C.J. Go on, go on, in God's name: but give us nothing that is impertinent.

Att. Indeed, my lord, I will keep to my matter. But, gentlemen, having now shown you, as I think, enough of this first meeting between the murdered person and the prisoner, I will shorten my tale so far as to say that from then on there were frequent meetings of the two: for the young woman was greatly tickled with having got hold (as she conceived it) of so likely a sweetheart, and he being once a week at least in the habit of passing through the street where she lived, she would be always on the watch for him; and it seems they had a signal arranged: he should whistle the tune that was played at the tavern: it is a tune, as I am informed, well known in that country, and has a burden, '*Madam, will you walk, will you talk with me?*'

L.C.J. Ay, I remember it in my own country, in Shropshire. It runs somehow thus, doth it not? [Here his lordship whistled a part of a tune, which was very observable, and seemed below the dignity of the court. And it appears he felt it so himself; for he said]: But this is by the mark, and I doubt it is the first time we have had dance-tunes in this court. The most part of the dancing we give occasion for is done at Tyburn. [Looking at the prisoner, who appeared very much disordered.] You said the tune was material to your case, Mr. Attorney, and upon my life I think Mr. Martin agrees with you. What ails you, man? staring like a player that sees a ghost!

Pris. My lord, I was amazed at hearing such trivial, foolish things as they bring against me.

L.C.J. Well, well, it lies upon Mr. Attorney to show whether they be trivial or not: but I must say, if he has nothing worse than this he has said, you have no great cause to be in amaze. Doth it not lie something deeper? But go on, Mr. Attorney.

Att. My lord and gentlemen – all that I have said so far you may indeed very reasonably reckon as having an appearance of triviality. And, to be sure, had the matter gone no further than the humouring of a poor silly girl by a young gentleman of quality, it had been very well. But to proceed. We shall make it appear that after three or four weeks the prisoner became contracted to a young gentlewoman of that country, one suitable every way to his own condition, and such an arrangement was on foot that seemed to promise him a happy and a reputable living. But within no very long time it seems that this young gentlewoman, hearing of the jest that was going about that countryside with regard to the prisoner and Ann Clark, conceived that it was not only an unworthy carriage on the part of her lover, but a derogation to herself that he should suffer his name to be sport for tavern company: and so without more ado she, with the consent of her parents, signified to the prisoner that the match between them was at an end. We shall show you that upon the receipt of this intelligence the prisoner was greatly enraged against Ann Clark as being the cause of his misfortune, (though indeed there was nobody answerable for it but himself,) and that he made use of many outrageous expressions and threatenings against her, and subsequently upon meeting with her both abused her and struck at her with his whip: but she, being but a poor innocent, could not be persuaded to desist from her attachment to him, but would often run after him testifying with gestures and broken words the affection she had to him: until she was become, as he said, the very plague of his life. Yet, being that affairs in which he was now engaged necessarily took him by the house in which she lived, he could not (as I am willing to believe he would otherwise have done) avoid meeting with her from time to time. We shall further show you that this was the posture of things up to the 15th day of May in this present year. Upon that day the prisoner comes riding through the village, as of custom, and met with the young woman: but in place of passing her by, as he had lately done, he stopped, and said some words to her with which she appeared wonderfully pleased, and so left her; and after that day she was nowhere to be found, not withstanding a strict search was made for her. The next time of the prisoner's passing through the place, her relations inquired of him whether he should know anything of her whereabouts; which he totally denied. They expressed to him their fears lest her weak intellects should have been upset by the attention he had showed her, and so she might have committed some rash act against her own life, calling him to witness the same time how often they had beseeched him to desist from taking notice of her, as fearing trouble might come of it: but this, too, he easily laughed away. But in spite of this light behaviour, it was noticeable in him that about this time his carriage and demeanour changed, and it was said of him that he seemed a troubled man. And here I come to a passage to which I should not dare to ask your attention, but that it appears to me to be founded in truth, and is supported by testimony deserving of credit. And, gentlemen, to my judgment it doth afford a great instance of God's revenge against murder, and that He will require the blood of the innocent.

[Here Mr. Attorney made a pause, and shifted with his papers: and it was thought remarkable by me and others, because he was a man not easily dashed.]

L.C.J. Well, Mr. Attorney, what is your instance?
Att. My lord, it is a strange one, and the truth is that, of all the cases I have been concerned in, I cannot call to mind the like of it. But to be short, gentlemen, we shall bring you testimony that Ann Clark was seen after this 15th of May, and that, at such time as she was so seen, it was impossible she could have been a living person.

[Here the people made a hum, and a good deal of laughter, and the Court called for silence, and when it was made]—

L.C.J. Why, Mr. Attorney, you might save up this tale for a week; it will be Christmas by that time, and you can frighten your cook-maids with it [at which the people laughed again, and the prisoner also, as it seemed]. God, man, what are you prating of – ghosts and Christmas jigs and tavern company – and here is a man's life at stake! (To the prisoner): And you, sir, I would have you know there is not so much occasion for you to make merry neither. You were not brought here for that, and if I know Mr. Attorney, he has more in his brief than he has shown yet. Go on, Mr. Attorney. I need not, mayhap, have spoken so sharply, but you must confess your course is something unusual.

Att. Nobody knows it better than I, my lord: but I shall bring it to an end with a round turn. I shall show you, gentlemen, that Ann Clark's body was found in the month of June, in a pond of water, with the throat cut: that a knife belonging to the prisoner was found in the same water: that he made efforts to recover the said knife from the water: that the coroner's quest brought in a verdict against the prisoner at the bar, and that therefore he should by course have been tried at Exeter: but that, suit being made on his behalf, on account that an impartial jury could not be found to try him in his own country, he hath had that singular favour shown him that he should be tried here in London. And so we will proceed to call our evidence.

Then the facts of the acquaintance between the prisoner and Ann Clark were proved, and also the coroner's inquest. I pass over this portion of the trial, for it offers nothing of special interest.

Sarah Arscott was next called and sworn.

Att. What is your occupation?

S. I keep the New Inn at —.

Att. Do you know the prisoner at the bar?

S. Yes: he was often at our house since he come first at Christmas of last year.

Att. Did you know Ann Clark?

S. Yes, very well.

Att. Pray, what manner of person was she in her appearance?

S. She was a very short thick-made woman: I do not know what else you would have me say.

Att. Was she comely?

S. No, not by no manner of means: she was very uncomely, poor child! She had a great face and hanging chops and a very bad colour like a puddock.

L.C.J. What is that, mistress? What say you she was like?

S. My lord, I ask pardon; I heard Esquire Martin say she looked like a puddock in the face; and so she did.

L.C.J. Did you that? Can you interpret her, Mr. Attorney?

Att. My lord, I apprehend it is the country word for a toad.

L.C.J. Oh, a hop-toad! Ay, go on.

Att. Will you give an account to the jury of what passed between you and the prisoner at the bar in May last?

S. Sir, it was this. It was about nine o'clock the evening after that Ann did not come home, and I was about my work in the house; there was no company there only Thomas Snell, and it was foul weather. Esquire Martin came in and called for some drink, and I, by way of pleasantry, I said to him, "Squire, have you been looking after your sweetheart?' and he flew out at me in a passion and desired I would not use such expressions. I was amazed at that, because we were accustomed to joke with him about her.

L.C.J. Who, her?

S. Ann Clark, my lord. And we had not heard the news of his being contracted to a young gentlewoman elsewhere, or I am sure I should have used better manners. So I said nothing, but being I was a little put out, I begun singing, to myself as it were, the song they danced to the first time they met, for I thought it would prick him. It was the same that he was used to sing when he come down the street; I have heard it very often: '*Madam, will you walk, will you talk with me?*' And it fell out that I needed something that was in the kitchen. So I went out to get it, and all the time I went on singing, something louder and more bold-like. And as I was there all of a sudden I thought I heard some one answering outside the house, but I could not be sure because of the wind blowing so high. So then I stopped singing, and now I heard it plain, saying, '*Yes, sir, I will walk, I will talk with you,*' and I knew the voice for Ann Clark's voice.

Att. How did you know it to be her voice?

S. It was impossible I could be mistaken. She had a dreadful voice, a kind of a squalling voice, in particular if she tried to sing. And there was nobody in the village that could counterfeit it, for they often tried. Sc, hearing that, I was glad, because we were all in an anxiety to know what was gone with her: for though she was a natural, she had a good disposition and was very tractable: and says I to myself, 'What, child! are you returned, then?' and I ran into the front room, and said to Squire Martin as I passed by, 'Squire, here is your sweetheart back again: shall I call her in?' and with that I went to open the door; but Squire Martin he caught hold of me, and it seemed to me he was out of his wits, or near upon. 'Hold, woman,' says he, 'in God's name!' and I know not what else: he was all of a shake. Then I was angry, and said I, 'What! are you not glad that poor child is found?' and I called to Thomas Snell and said, 'If the Squire will not let me, do you open the door and call her in.' So Thomas Snell went and opened the door, and the wind setting that way blew in and overset the two candles that was all we had lighted: and Esquire Martin fell away from holding me; I think he fell down on the floor, but we were wholly in the dark, and it was a minute or two before I got a light again: and while I was feeling for the fire-box, I am not certain but I heard some one step 'cross the floor, and I am sure I heard the door of the great cupboard that stands in the room open and shut to. Then, when I had a light again, I see Esquire Martin on the settle, all white and sweaty as if he had swounded away, and his arms hanging down; and I was going to help him; but just then it caught my eye that there was something like a bit of a dress shut into the cupboard door, and it came to my mind I had heard that door shut. So I thought it might be some person had run in when the light was quenched, and was hiding in the cupboard. So I went up closer and looked: and there was a bit of a black stuff cloak, and just below it an edge of a brown stuff dress, both sticking out of the shut of the door: and both of them was low down, as if the person that had them on might be crouched down inside.

Att. What did you take it to be?

S. I took it to be a woman's dress.

Att. Could you make any guess whom it belonged to? Did you know any one who wore such a dress?

S. It was a common stuff, by what I could see. I have seen many women wearing such a stuff in our parish.

Att. Was it like Ann Clark's dress?

S. She used to wear just such a dress: but I could not say on my oath it was hers.

Att. Did you observe anything else about it?

S. I did notice that it looked very wet: but it was foul weather outside.

L.C.J. Did you feel of it, mistress?

S. No, my lord, I did not like to touch it.

L.C.J. Not like? Why that? Are you so nice that you scruple to feel of a wet dress?

S. Indeed, my lord, I cannot very well tell why: only it had a nasty ugly look about it.

L.C.J. Well, go on.

S. Then I called again to Thomas Snell, and bid him come to me and catch any one that come out when I should open the cupboard door, 'for,' says I, 'there is some one hiding within, and I would know what she wants.' And with that Squire Martin gave a sort of a cry or a shout and ran out of the house into the dark, and I felt the cupboard door pushed out against me while I held it, and Thomas Snell helped me: but for all we pressed to keep it shut as hard as we could, it was forced out against us, and we had to fall back.

L.C.J. And pray what came out – a mouse?

S. No, my lord, it was greater than a mouse, but I could not see what it was: it fleeted very swift over the floor and out at the door.

L.C.J. But come; what did it look like? Was it a person?

S. My lord, I cannot tell what it was, but it ran very low, and it was of a dark colour. We were both daunted by it, Thomas Snell and I, but we made all the haste we could after it to the door that stood open. And we looked out, but it was dark and we could see nothing.

L.C.J. Was there no tracks of it on the floor? What floor have you there?

S. It is a flagged floor and sanded, my lord, and there was an appearance of a wet track on the floor, but we could make nothing of it, neither Thomas Snell nor me, and besides, as I said, it was a foul night.

L.C.J. Well, for my part, I see not – though to be sure it is an odd tale she tells – what you would do with this evidence.

Att. My lord, we bring it to show the suspicious carriage of the prisoner immediately after the disappearance of the murdered person: and we ask the jury's consideration of that; and also to the matter of the voice heard without the house.

Then the prisoner asked some questions not very material, and Thomas Snell was next called, who gave evidence to the same effect as Mrs. Arscott, and added the following:—

Att. Did anything pass between you and the prisoner during the time Mrs. Arscott was out of the room?

Th. I had a piece of twist in my pocket.

Att. Twist of what?

Th. Twist of tobacco, sir, and I felt a disposition to take a pipe of tobacco. So I found a pipe on the chimney-piece, and being it was twist, and in regard of me having by an oversight left my knife at my house, and me not having over many teeth to pluck at it, as your lordship or any one else may have a view by their own eyesight—

L.C.J. What is the man talking about? Come to the matter, fellow! Do you think we sit here to look at your teeth?

Th. No, my lord, nor I would not you should do, God forbid! I know your honours have better employment, and better teeth, I would not wonder.

L.C.J. Good God, what a man is this! Yes, I *have* better teeth, and that you shall find if you keep not to the purpose.

Th. I humbly ask pardon, my lord, but so it was. And I took upon me, thinking no harm, to ask Squire Martin to lend me his knife to cut my tobacco. And he felt first of one pocket and then of another and it was not there at all. And says I, 'What! have you lost your knife, Squire?' And up he gets and feels again and he sat down, and such a groan as he gave, 'Good God!' he says, 'I must have left it there.' 'But,' says I, 'Squire, by all appearance it is *not* there. Did you set a value on it,' says I, 'you might have it cried.' But he sat there and put his head between his hands and seemed to take no notice to what I said. And then it was Mistress Arscott come tracking back out of the kitchen place.

Asked if he heard the voice singing outside the house, he said 'No,' but the door into the kitchen was shut, and there was a high wind: but says that no one could mistake Ann Clark's voice.

Then a boy, William Reddaway, about thirteen years of age, was called, and by the usual questions, put by the Lord Chief Justice, it was ascertained that he knew the nature of an oath. And so he was sworn. His evidence referred to a time about a week later.

Att. Now, child, don't be frighted: there is no one here will hurt you if you speak the truth.

L. C.J. Ay, if he speak the truth. But remember, child, thou art in the presence of the great God of heaven and earth, that hath the keys of hell, and of us that are the king's officers, and have the keys of Newgate; and remember, too, there is a man's life in question; and if thou tellest a lie, and by that means he comes to an ill end, thou art no better than his murderer; and so speak the truth.

Att. Tell the jury what you know, and speak out. Where were you on the evening of the 23rd of May last?

L. C.J. Why, what does such a boy as this know of days. Can you mark the day, boy?

W. Yes, my lord, it was the day before our feast, and I was to spend sixpence there, and that falls a month before Midsummer Day.

One of the Jury. My lord, we cannot hear what he says.

L. C.J. He says he remembers the day because it was the day before the feast they had there, and he had sixpence to lay out. Set him up on the table there. Well, child, and where wast thou then?

W. Keeping cows on the moor, my lord.

But, the boy using the country speech, my lord could not well apprehend him, and so asked if there was any one that could interpret him, and it was answered the parson of the parish was there, and he was accordingly sworn and so the evidence given. The boy said—

'I was on the moor about six o'clock, and sitting behind a bush of furze near a pond of water: and the prisoner came very cautiously and looking about him, having something like a long pole in his hand, and stopped a good while as if he would be listening, and then began to feel in the water with the pole: and I being very near the water – not above five yards – heard as if the pole struck up against something that made a wallowing sound, and the prisoner dropped the pole and threw himself on the ground, and rolled himself about very strangely with his hands to his ears, and so after a while got up and went creeping away.'

Asked if he had had any communication with the prisoner, 'Yes, a day or two before, the prisoner, hearing I was used to be on the moor, he asked me if I had seen a knife laying about, and said he would give sixpence to find it. And I said I had not seen any such thing, but I would ask about. Then he said he would give me sixpence to say nothing, and so he did.

L.C.J. And was that the sixpence you were to lay out at the feast?
W. Yes, if you please, my lord.

Asked if he had observed anything particular as to the pond of water, he said, 'No, except that it begun to have a very ill smell and the cows would not drink of it for some days before.'

Asked if he had ever seen the prisoner and Ann Clark in company together, he began to cry very much, and it was a long time before they could get him to speak intelligibly. At last the parson of the parish, Mr. Matthews, got him to be quiet, and the question being put to him again, he said he had seen Ann Clark waiting on the moor for the prisoner at some way off, several times since last Christmas.

Att. Did you see her close, so as to be sure it was she?
W. Yes, quite sure.
L.C.J. How quite sure, child?
W. Because she would stand and jump up and down and clap her arms like a goose (which he called by some country name: but the parson explained it to be a goose). And then she was of such a shape that it could not be no one else.
Att. What was the last time that you so saw her?

Then the witness began to cry again and clung very much to Mr. Matthews, who bid him not be frightened. And so at last he told this story: that on the day before their feast (being the same evening that he had before spoken of) after the prisoner had gone away, it being then twilight and he very desirous to get home, but afraid for the present to stir from where he was lest the prisoner should see him, remained some few minutes behind the bush, looking on the pond, and saw something dark come up out of the water at the edge of the pond furthest away from him, and so up the bank. And when it got to the top where he could see it plain against the sky, it stood up and flapped the arms up and down, and then run off very swiftly in the same direction the prisoner had taken: and being asked very strictly who he took it to be, he said upon his oath that it could be nobody but Ann Clark.

Thereafter his master was called, and gave evidence that the boy had come home very late that evening and been chided for it, and that he seemed very much amazed, but could give no account of the reason.

Att. My lord, we have done with our evidence for the King.

Then the Lord Chief Justice called upon the prisoner to make his defence; which he did, though at no great length, and in a very halting way, saying that he hoped the jury would not go about to take his life on the evidence of a parcel of country people and children that would believe any idle tale; and that he had been very much prejudiced in his trial; at which the L.C.J. interrupted him, saying that he had had singular favour shown to him in having his trial removed from Exeter, which the prisoner acknowledging, said that he meant rather that since he was brought to London there had not been care taken to keep him secured from interruption and disturbance. Upon which the L.C.J. ordered the Marshal to be called, and questioned him about the safe keeping of the prisoner, but could find nothing: except the Marshal said that he had been informed by the underkeeper that they had seen a person outside his door or going up the stairs to it: but there was no possibility the person should have got in. And it being inquired further what sort of person this might be, the Marshal could not speak to it save by hearsay, which was not allowed. And the prisoner, being asked if this was what he meant, said no, he knew nothing of that, but it was very hard that a man should not be suffered to be at quiet when his life stood on it. But it was observed he was very hasty in his denial. And so he said no more, and called no witnesses. Whereupon the Attorney-General spoke to the jury. [A full report of what he said is given, and, if time allowed, I would extract that portion in which he dwells on the alleged appearance of the murdered person: he quotes some authorities of ancient date, as St. Augustine *de cura pro mortuis gerenda* (a favourite book of reference with the old writers on the supernatural) and also cites some cases which may be seen in Glanvil's, but more conveniently in Mr. Lang's books. He does not, however, tell us more of those cases than is to be found in print.]

The Lord Chief Justice then summed up the evidence for the jury. His speech, again, contains nothing that I find worth copying out: but he was naturally impressed with the singular character of the evidence, saying that he had never heard such given in his experience; but that there was nothing in law to set it aside, and that the jury must consider whether they believed these witnesses or not.

And the jury after a very short consultation brought the prisoner in Guilty.

So he was asked whether he had anything to say in arrest of judgment, and pleaded that his name was spelt wrong in the indictment, being Martin with an I, whereas it should be with a Y. But this was overruled as not material, Mr. Attorney saying, moreover, that he could bring evidence to show that the prisoner by times wrote it as it was laid in the indictment. And, the prisoner having nothing further to offer, sentence of death was passed upon him, and that he should be hanged in chains upon a gibbet near the place where the fact was committed, and that execution should take place upon the 28th December next ensuing, being Innocents' Day.

Thereafter the prisoner being to all appearance in a state of desperation, made shift to ask the L.C.J. that his relations might be allowed to come to him during the short time he had to live.

L.C.J. Ay, with all my heart, so it be in the presence of the keeper; and Ann Clark may come to you as well, for what I care.

At which the prisoner broke out and cried to his lordship not to use such words to him, and his lordship very angrily told him he deserved no tenderness at any man's hands for a cowardly butcherly murderer that had not the stomach to take the reward of his deeds: 'and I hope to God,' said he, 'that she *will* be with you by day and by night till an end is made of you.' Then the prisoner was removed, and, so far as I saw, he was in a swound, and the court broke up.

I cannot refrain from observing that the prisoner during all the time of the trial seemed to be more uneasy than is commonly the case even in capital causes: that, for example, he was looking narrowly among the people and often turning round very sharply, as if some person might be at his ear. It was also very noticeable at this trial what a silence the people kept, and further (though this might not be otherwise than natural in that season of the year), what a darkness and obscurity there was in the court room, lights being brought in not long after two o'clock in the day, and yet no fog in the town.

★

It was not without interest that I heard lately from some young men who had been giving a concert in the village I speak of, that a very cold reception was accorded to the song which has been mentioned in this narrative: '*Madam, will you walk?*' It came out in some talk they had next morning with some of the local people that that song was regarded with an invincible repugnance – it was not so, they believed, at North Tawton – but here it was reckoned to be unlucky. However, why that view was taken no one had the shadow of an idea.

"OH, WHISTLE, AND I'LL COME TO YOU, MY LAD"

"I suppose you will be getting away pretty soon, now Full term is over, Professor," said a person not in the story to the Professor of Ontography, soon after they had sat down next to each other at a feast in the hospitable hall of St. James's College.

The Professor was young, neat, and precise in speech.

"Yes," he said; "my friends have been making me take up golf this term, and I mean to go to the East Coast – in point of fact to Burnstow (I dare say you know it) – for a week or ten days, to improve my game. I hope to get off tomorrow."

"Oh, Parkins," said his neighbour on the other side, "if you are going to Burnstow, I wish you would look at the site of the Templars' preceptory, and let me know if you think it would be any good to have a dig there in the summer."

It was, as you might suppose, a person of antiquarian pursuits who said this, but, since he merely appears in this prologue, there is no need to give his entitlements.

"Certainly," said Parkins, the Professor: "if you will describe to me whereabouts the site is, I will do my best to give you an idea of the lie of the land when I get back, or I could write to you about it, if you would tell me where you are likely to be."

"Don't trouble to do that, thanks. It's only that I'm thinking of taking my family in that direction in the Long, and it occurred to me that, as very few of the English preceptories have ever been properly planned, I might have an opportunity of doing something useful on off-days."

The Professor rather sniffed at the idea that planning out a preceptory could be described as useful. His neighbour continued :

"The site – I doubt if there is anything showing above ground – must be down quite close to the beach now. The sea has encroached tremendously, as you know, all along that bit of coast. I should think, from the map, that it must be about three-quarters of a mile from the Globe Inn, at the north end of the town. Where are you going to stay?"

"Well, *at* the Globe Inn, as a matter of fact," said Parkins. "I have engaged a room there. I couldn't get in anywhere else; most of the lodging-houses are shut up in winter, it seems; and, as it is, they tell me that the only room of any size I can have is really a double-bedded one, and that they haven't a corner in which to store the other bed, and so on. But I must have a fairly large room, for I am taking some books down, and mean to do a bit of work; and though I don't quite fancy having an empty bed – not to speak of two – in what I may call for the time being my study, I suppose I can manage to rough it for the short time I shall be there."

"Do you call having an extra bed in your room roughing it, Parkins?" said a bluff person opposite. "Look here, I shall come down and occupy it for a bit; it'll be company for you."

The Professor quivered, but managed to laugh in a courteous manner.

"By all means, Rogers; there's nothing I should like better. But I'm afraid you would find it rather dull; you don't play golf, do you?"

"No, thank Heaven!" said rude Mr. Rogers.

"Well, you see, when I'm not writing I shall most likely be out on the links, and that, as I say, would be rather dull for you, I'm afraid."

"Oh, I don't know! There's certain to be somebody I know in the place; but, of course, if you don't want me, speak the word, Parkins; I shan't be offended. Truth, as you always tell us, is never offensive."

Parkins was, indeed, scrupulously polite and strictly truthful. It is to be feared that Mr. Rogers sometimes practised upon his knowledge of these characteristics. In Parkins's breast there was a conflict now raging, which for a moment or two did not allow him to answer. That interval being over, he said :

"Well, if you want the exact truth, Rogers, I was considering whether the room I speak of would really be large enough to accommodate us both comfortably; and also whether (mind, I shouldn't have said this if you hadn't pressed me) you would not constitute something in the nature of a hindrance to my work."

Rogers laughed loudly.

"Well done, Parkins!" he said. "It's all right. I promise not to interrupt your work; don't you disturb yourself about that. No, I won't come if you don't want me; but I thought I should do so nicely to keep the ghosts off." Here he might have been seen to wink and to nudge his next neighbour. Parkins might also have been seen to become pink. "I beg pardon, Parkins," Rogers continued; "I oughtn't to have said that. I forgot you didn't like levity on these topics."

"Well," Parkins said, "as you have mentioned the matter, I freely own that I do *not* like careless talk about what you call ghosts. A man in my position," he went on, raising his voice a little, "cannot, I find, be too careful about appearing to sanction the current beliefs on such subjects. As you know, Rogers, or as you ought to know; for I think I have never concealed my views – "

"No, you certainly have not, old man," put in Rogers *sotto voce.*

" – I hold that any semblance, any appearance of concession to the view that such things might exist is equivalent to a renunciation of all that I hold most sacred. But I'm afraid I have not succeeded in securing your attention."

"Your *undivided* attention, was what Dr. Blimber actually *said*,"[1] Rogers interrupted, with every appearance of an earnest desire for accuracy. "But I beg your pardon, Parkins: I'm stopping you."

"No, not at all," said Parkins. "I don't remember Blimber; perhaps he was before my time. But I needn't go on. I'm sure you know what I mean."

"Yes, yes," said Rogers, rather hastily – "just so. We'll go into it fully at Burnstow, or somewhere."

In repeating the above dialogue I have tried to give the impression which it made on me, that Parkins was something of an old woman – rathen hen-like, perhaps, in his little ways; totally destitute, alas! of the sense of humour, but at the same time dauntless and sincere in his convictions, and a man deserving of the greatest respect. Whether or not the reader has gathered so much, that was the character which Parkins had.

On the following day Parkins did, as he had hoped, succeed in getting away from his college, and in arriving at Burnstow. He was made welcome at the Globe Inn, was safely installed in the large double-bedded room of which we have heard, and was able before retiring to rest to arrange his material for work in apple-pie order upon a commodious table which occupied the outer end of the room, and was surrounded on three sides by windows looking out seaward; that is to say, the central window looked straight out to sea, and those on the left and right com-

[1] Mr. Rogers was wrong, *vide Dombey and Son*, chapter xii.

manded prospects along the shore to the north and south respectively. On the south you saw the village of Burnstow. On the north no houses were to be seen, but only the beach and the low cliff backing it. Immediately in front was a strip – not considerable – of rough grass, dotted with old anchors, capstans, and so forth; then a broad path; then the beach. Whatever may have been the original distance between the Globe Inn and the sea, not more than sixty yards now separated them.

The rest of the population of the inn was, of course, a golfing one, and included few elements that call for a special description. The most conspicuous figure was, perhaps, that of an *ancien militaire*, secretary of a London club, and possessed of a voice of incredible strength, and of view of a pronouncedly Protestant type. These were apt to find utterance after his attendance upon the ministrations of the Vicar, an estimable man with inclinations towards a picturesque ritual, which he gallantly kept down as far as he could out of deference to East Anglian tradition.

Professor Parkins, one of whose principal characteristics was pluck, spent the greater part of the day following his arrival at Burnstow in what he had called improving his game, in company with this Colonel Wilson : and during the afternoon – whether the process of improvement were to blame or not, I am not sure – the Colonel's demeanour assumed a colouring so lurid that even Parkins jibbed at the thought of walking home with him from the links. He determined, after a short and furtive look at that bristling moustache and those incarnadined features, that it would be wiser to allow the influence of tea and tobacco to do what they could with the Colonel before the dinner-hour should render a meeting inevitable.

"I might walk home tonight along the beach," he reflected – "yes, and take a look – there will be light enough for that – at the ruins of which Disney was talking. I don't exactly know where they are, by the way; but I expect I can hardly help stumbling on them."

This he accomplished, I may say, in the most literal sense, for in picking his way from the links to the shingle beach his foot caught, partly in a gorse-root and partly in a biggish stone, and over he went. When he got up and surveyed his surroundings, he found himself in a patch of somewhat broken ground covered with small depressions and mounds. These latter, when he came to examine them, proved to be simply masses of flints embedded in mortar and grown over with turf. He must, he quite rightly concluded, be on the site of the preceptory he had promised to look at. It seemed not unlikely to reward the spade of the explorer; enough of the foundations was probably left at no great depth to throw a good deal of light on the general plan. He remembered vaguely that the Templars, to whom this site had belonged, were in the habit of building round churches, and he thought a particular series of the humps or mounds near him did appear to be arranged in something of a circular form. Few people can resist the temptation to try a little amateur research in a department quite outside their own, if only for the satisfaction of showing how successful they would have been had they only taken it up seriously. Our Professor, however, if he felt something of this mean desire, was also truly anxious to oblige Mr. Disney. So he paced with care the circular area he had noticed, and wrote down its rough dimensions in his pocket-book. Then he proceeded to examine an oblong eminence which lay east of the centre of the circle, and seemed to his thinking likely to be the base of a platform or altar. At one end of it, the northern, a patch of the turf was gone – removed by some boy or other creature *feræ naturæ*. It might, he thought, be as well to probe the soil here for evidences of masonry, and he took out his knife and began scraping away the earth. And now followed another little discovery : a portion of soil fell inward as he scraped, and disclosed a small cavity. He lighted one match after another to help him to see of what nature the hole was, but the wind was too strong for them all. By tapping and scratching the sides with his knife, however, he was able to make out that it must be an artficial hole in masonry. It was rectangular, and the sides, top, and bottom, if not actually plastered, were smooth and regular. Of course it was empty. No! As he withdrew the knife he heard a metallic clink, and when he introduced his hand it met with a cylindrical object lying on the floor of the hole. Naturally enough, he picked it up, and when he brought it into the light, now fast fading, he could see that it, too, was of man's making – a metal tube about four inches long and evidently of some considerable age.

By the time Parkins had made sure that there was nothing else in this odd receptacle, it was too late and too dark for him to think of undertaking any further search. What he had done had proved so unexpectedly interesting that he determined to sacrifice a little more of the daylight on the morrow to archæology. The object which he now had' safe in his pocket was bound to be of some slight value at least, he felt sure.

Bleak and solemn was the view on which he took a last look before starting homeward. A faint yellow light in the west showed the links, on which a few figures moving towards the club-house were still visible, the squat martello tower, the lights of Aldsey village, the pale ribbon of sands intersected at intervals by black wooden groynes, the dim and murmuring sea. The wind was bitter from the north, but was at his back when he set out for the Globe. He quickly rattled and clashed through the shingle and gained the sand, upon which, but for the groynes which had to be got over every few yards, the going was both good and quiet. One last look behind, to measure the distance he had made since leaving the ruined Templars' church, showed him a prospect of company on his walk, in the shape of a rather indistinct personage, who seemed to be making great efforts to catch up with him, but made little, if any, progress. I mean that there was an appearance of running about his movements, but that the distance between him and Parkins did not seem materially to lessen. So, at least, Parkins thought, and decided that he almost certainly did not know him, and that it would be absurd to wait until he came up. For all that, company, he began to think, would really be very welcome on that lonely shore, if only you could choose your companion. In his unenlightened days he had read of meetings in such places which even now would hardly bear thinking of. He went on thinking of them, however, until he reached home, and particularly of one which catches most people's fancy at some time of their childhood. "Now I saw in my dream that Christian had gone but a very little way when he saw a foul fiend coming over the field to meet him." "What should I do now," he thought, "if I looked back and caught sight of a black figure sharply defined against the yellow sky, and saw that it had horns and wings? I wonder whether I should stand or run for it. Luckily, the gentleman behind is not of that kind, and he seems to be about as far off now as when I saw him first. Well, at this rate he won't get his dinner as soon as I shall; and, dear me! it's within a quarter of an hour of the time now. I must run!"

Parkins had, in fact, very little time for dressing. When he met the Colonel at dinner, Peace – or as much of her as that gentleman could manage – reigned once more in the military bosom; nor was she put to flight in the hours of bridge that followed dinner, for Parkins was a more than respectable player. When, therefore, he retired towards twelve o'clock, he felt that he had spent his evening in quite a satisfactory way, and that, even for so long as a fortnight or three weeks, life at the Globe would be supportable under similar conditions – "especially," thought he, "if I go on improving my game."

As he went along the passages he met the boots of the Globe, who stopped and said :

"Beg your pardon, sir, but as I was a-brushing your coat just now there was somethink fell out of the pocket. I put it on your chest of drawers, sir, in your room, sir – a piece of a pipe or somethink of that, sir. Thank you, sir. You'll find it on your chest of drawers, sir – yes, sir. Good night, sir."

The speech served to remind Parkins of his little discovery of that afternoon. It was with some considerable curiosity that he turned it over by the light of his candles. It was of bronze, he now saw, and was shaped very much after the manner of the modern dog-whistle; in fact it was – yes, certainly it was – actually no more nor less than a whistle. He put it to his lips, but it was quite full of a fine, caked-up sand or earth, which would not yield to knocking, but must be loosened with a knife. Tidy as ever in his habits, Parkins cleared out the earth on to a piece of paper, and took the latter to the window to empty it out. The night was clear and bright, as he saw when he had opened the casement, and he stopped for an instant to look at the sea and note a belated wanderer stationed on the shore in front of the inn. Then he shut the window, a little surprised at the late hours people kept at Burnstow, and took his whistle to the light again. Why, surely there were marks on it, and not merely marks, but letters! A very little rubbing rendered the deeply-cut inscription quite legible, but the Professor had to confess, after some earnest thought, that the meaning of it was as obscure to him as the writing on the wall to Belshazzar. There were legends both on the front and on the back of the whistle. The one read thus :

$$\text{FUR} \quad \begin{array}{c} \text{PLA} \\ \text{FLE} \end{array} \quad \text{BIS}$$

The other :

$$\maltese \text{ QUIS EST ISTE QUI UENIT } \maltese$$

119

"I ought to be able to make it out," he thought; "but I suppose I am a little rusty in my Latin. When I come to think of it, I don't believe I even know the word for a whistle. The long one does seem simple enough. It ought to mean, 'Who is this who is coming?' Well, the best way to find out is evidently to whistle for him."

He blew tentatively and stopped suddenly, startled and yet pleased at the note he had elicited. It had a quality of infinite distance in it, and, soft as it was, he somehow felt it must be audible for miles round. It was sound, too, that seemed to have the power (which many scents possess) of forming pictures in the brain. He saw quite clearly for a moment a vision of a wide, dark expanse at night, with a fresh wind blowing, and in the midst a lonely figure – how employed, he could not tell. Perhaps he would have seen more had not the picture been broken by the sudden surge of a gust of wind against his casement, so sudden that it made him look up, just in time to see the white glint of a sea-bird's wing somewhere outside the dark panes.

The sound of the whistle had so fascinated him that he could not help trying it once more, this time more boldly. The note was little, if at all, louder than before, and repetition broke the illusion – no picture followed, as he had half hoped it might. "But what is this? Goodness! what force the wind can get up in a few minutes! What a tremendous gust! There! I knew that window-fastening was no use! Ah! I thought so – both candles out. It's enough to tear the room to pieces."

The first thing was to get the window shut. While you might count twenty Parkins was struggling with the small casement, and felt almost as if he were pushing back a sturdy burglar, so strong was the pressure. It slackened all at once, and the window banged to and latched itself. Now to relight the candles and see what damage, if any, had been done. No, nothing seemed amiss; no glass even was broken in the casement. But the noise had evidently roused at least one member of the household : the Colonel was to be heard stumping in his stockinged feet on the floor above, and growling.

Quickly as it had risen, the wind did not fall at once. On it went, moaning and rushing past the house, at times rising to a cry so desolate that, as Parkins disinterestedly said, it might have made fanciful people feel quite uncomfortable; even the unimaginative, he thought after a quarter of an hour, might be happier without it.

Whether it was the wind, or the excitement of golf, or of the researches in the preceptory that kept Parkins awake, he was not sure. Awake he remained, in any case, long enough to fancy (as I am afraid I often do myself under such conditions), that he was the victim of all manner of fatal disorders : he would lie counting the beats of his heart, convinced that it was going to stop work every moment, and would entertain grave suspicions of his lungs, brain, liver, etc. – suspicions which he was sure would be dispelled by the return of daylight, but which until then refused to be put aside. He found a little vicarious comfort in the idea that someone else was in the same boat. A near neighbour (in the darkness it was not easy to tell his direction) was tossing and rustling in his bed, too.

The next stage was that Parkins shut his eyes and determined to give sleep every chance. Here again overexcitement asserted itself in another form – that of making pictures. *Experto crede*, pictures do come to the closed eyes of one trying to sleep, and are often so little to his taste that he must open his eyes and disperse them.

Parkins's experience on this occasion was a very distressing one. He found that the picture which presented itself to him was continuous. When he opened his eyes, of course, it went; but when he shut them once more it framed itself afresh, and acted itself out again, neither quicker nor slower than before. What he saw was this :

A long stretch of shore – shingle edged by sand, and

intersected at short intervals with black groynes running down to the water – a scene, in fact, so like that of his afternoon's walk that, in the absence of any landmark, it could not be distinguished therefrom. The light was obscure, conveying an impression of gathering storm, late winter evening, and slight cold rain. On this bleak stage at first no actor was visible. Then, in the distance, a bobbing black object appeared; a moment more, and it was a man running, jumping, clambering over the groynes, and every few seconds looking eagerly back. The nearer he came the more obvious it was that he was not only anxious, but even terribly frightened, though his face was not to be distinguished. He was, moreover, almost at the end of his strength. On he came; each successive obstacle seemed to cause him more difficulty than the last. "Will he get over this next one?" thought Parkins; "it seems a little higher than the others." Yes; half climbing, half throwing himself, he did get over, and fell all in a heap on the other side (the side nearest to the spectator). There, as if really unable to get up again, he remained crouching under the groyne, looking up in an attitude of painful anxiety.

So far no cause whatever for the fear of the runner had been shown; but now there began to be seen, far up the shore, a little flicker of something light-coloured moving to and fro with great swiftness and irregularity. Rapidly growing larger, it, too, declared itself as a figure in pale, fluttering draperies, ill-defined. There was something about its motion which made Parkins very unwilling to see it at close quarters. It would stop, raise arms, bow itself towards the sand, then run stooping across the beach to the water-edge and back again; and then, rising upright, once more continue its course forward at a speed that was startling and terrifying. The moment came when the pursuer was hovering about from left to right only a few yards beyond the groyne where the runner lay in hiding. After two or three ineffectual castings hither and thither it came to a stop, stood upright, with arms raised high, and then darted straight forward towards the groyne.

It was at this point that Parkins always failed in his resolution to keep his eyes shut. With many misgivings as to incipient failure of eyesight, over-worked brain, excessive smoking, and so on, he finally resigned himself to light his candle, get out a book, and pass the night waking, rather than be tormented by this persistent panorama, which he saw clearly enough could only be a morbid reflection of his walk and his thoughts on that very day.

The scraping of match on box and the glare of light must have startled some creatures of the night – rats or what not – which he heard scurry across the floor from the side of his bed with much rustling. Dear, dear! the match is out! Fool that it is! But the second one burnt better, and a candle and book were duly procured, over which Parkins pored till sleep of a wholesome kind came upon him, and that in no long space. For about the first time in his orderly and prudent life he forgot to blow out the candle, and when he was called next morning at eight there was still a flicker in the socket and a sad mess of guttered grease on the top of the little table.

After breakfast he was in his room, putting the finishing touches to his golfing costume – fortune had again allotted the Colonel to him for a partner – when one of the maids came in.

"Oh, if you please," she said, "would you like any extra blankets on your bed, sir?"

"Ah! thank you," said Parkins. "Yes, I think I should like one. It seems likely to turn rather colder."

In a very short time the maid was back with the blanket.

"Which bed should I put it on, sir?" she asked.

"What? Why, that one – the one I slept in last night," he said, pointing to it.

"Oh yes! I beg your pardon, sir, but you seemed to have

tried both of 'em; leastways, we had to make 'em both up this morning."

"Really? How very absurd!" said Parkins. "I certainly never touched the other, except to lay some things on it. Did it actually seem to have been slept in?"

"Oh yes, sir!" said the maid. "Why, all the things was crumpled and throwed about all ways, if you'll excuse me, sir – quite as if anyone 'adn't passed but a very poor night, sir."

"Dear me," said Parkins. "Well, I may have disordered it more than I thought when I unpacked my things. I'm very sorry to have given you the extra trouble, I'm sure. I expect a friend of mine soon, by the way – a gentleman from Cambridge – to come and occupy it for a night or two. That will be all right, I suppose, won't it?"

"Oh yes, to be sure, sir. Thank you, sir. It's no trouble, I'm sure," said the maid, and departed to giggle with her colleagues.

Parkins set forth, with a stern determination to improve his game.

I am glad to be able to report that he succeeded so far in this enterprise that the Colonel, who had been rather repining at the prospect of a second day's play in his company, became quite chatty as the morning advanced; and his voice boomed out over the flats, as certainly also of our own minor poets have said, "like some great bourdon in a minster tower".

"Extraordinary wind, that, we had last night," he said. "In my old home we should have said someone had been whistling for it."

"Should you, indeed!" said Parkins. "Is there a super-stition of that kind still current in your part of the country?"

"I don't know about superstition," said the Colonel. "They believe in it all over Denmark and Norway, as well as on the Yorkshire coast; and my experience is, mind you, that there's generally something at the bottom of what these country-folk hold to, and have held to for generations. But it's your drive" (or whatever it might have been : the golfing reader will have to imagine appropriate digressions at the proper intervals).

When conversation was resumed, Parkins said, with a slight hesitancy :

"Apropos of what you were saying just now, Colonel, I think I ought to tell you that my own views on such subjects are very strong. I am, in fact, a convinced disbeliever in what is called the 'supernatural'."

"What !" said the Colonel, "do you mean to tell me you don't believe in second-sight, or ghosts, or anything of that kind ?"

"In nothing whatever of that kind," returned Parkins firmly.

"Well," said the Colonel, "but it appears to me at that rate, sir, that you must be little better than a Sadducee."

Parkins was on the point of answering that, in his opinion, the Sadducees were the most sensible persons he had ever read of in the Old Testament; but, feeling some doubt as to whether much mention of them was to be found in that work, he preferred to laugh the accusation off.

"Perhaps I am," he said; "but – Here, give me my cleek, boy ! – Excuse me one moment, Colonel." A short interval. "Now, as to whistling for the wind, let me give you my theory about it. The laws which govern winds are really not at all perfectly known – to fisher-folk and such, of course, not known at all. A man or woman of eccentric habits, perhaps, or a stranger, is seen repeatedly on the beach at some unusual hour, and is heard whistling. Soon afterwards a violent wind rises; a man who could read the sky perfectly or who possessed a barometer could have foretold that it would. The simple people of a fishing-village have no barometers, and only a few rough rules for prophesying weather. What more natural than that the eccentric personage I postulated should be regarded as having raised the wind, or that he or she should clutch eagerly at the reputation of being able to do so? Now, take last night's wind : as it happens, I myself was whistling. I blew a whistle twice, and the wind seemed to come absolutely in answer to my call. If anyone had seen me – "

The audience had been a little restive under this harangue, and Parkins had, I fear, fallen somewhat into the tone of a lecturer; but at the last sentence the Colonel stopped.

"Whistling, were you?" he said. "And what sort of whistle did you use? Play this stroke first." Interval.

"About that whistle you were asking, Colonel. It's rather a curious one. I have it in my – No; I see I've left it in my room. As a matter of fact, I found it yesterday."

And then Parkins narrated the manner of his discovery of the whistle, upon hearing which the Colonel grunted, and opined that, in Parkins's place, he should himself be careful about using a thing that had belonged to a set of Papists, of whom, speaking generally, it might be affirmed that you never knew what they might not have been up to. From this topic he diverged to the enormities of the Vicar, who had given notice on the previous Sunday that Friday would be the Feast of St. Thomas the Apostle, and that there would be service at eleven o'clock in the church. This and other similar proceedings constituted in the Colonel's view a strong presumption that the Vicar was a concealed Papist, if not a Jesuit; and Parkins, who could not very readily follow the Colonel in this region, did not disagree with him. In fact, they got on so well together in the morning that there was no talk on either side of their separating after lunch.

Both continued to play well during the afternoon, or, at least, well enough to make them forget everything else until the light began to fail them. Not until then did Parkins remember that he had meant to do some more investigating at the preceptory; but it was of no great importance, he reflected. One day was as good as another; he might as well go home with the Colonel.

As they turned the corner of the house, the Colonel was almost knocked down by a boy who rushed into him at the very top of his speed, and then, instead of running away, remained hanging on to him and panting. The first words of the warrior were naturally those of reproof and objurgation, but he very quickly discerned that the boy was almost speechless with fright. Inquiries were useless at first. When the boy got his breath he began to howl, and still clung to the Colonel's legs. He was at last detached, but continued to howl.

"What in the world *is* the matter with you? What have you been up to? What have you seen?" said the two men.

"Ow, I seen it wive at me out of the winder," wailed the boy, "and I don't like it."

"What window?" said the irritated Colonel. "Come, pull yourself together, my boy."

"The front winder it was, at the 'otel," said the boy.

At this point Parkins was in favour of sending the boy home, but the Colonel refused; he wanted to get to the bottom of it, he said; it was most dangerous to give a boy such a fright as this one had had, and if it turned out that people had been playing jokes, they should suffer for it in some way. And by a series of questions he made out this story : The boy had been playing about on the grass in front of the Globe with some others; then they had gone home to their teas, and he was just going, when he happened to look up at the front winder and see it a-wiving at him. *It* seemed to be a figure of some sort, in white as far as he knew – couldn't see its face; but it wived at him, and it warn't a right thing – not to say not a right person. Was there a light in the room? No, he didn't think to look if there was a light. Which was the window? Was it the top one or the second one? The seckind one it was – the big winder what got two little uns at the sides.

"Very well, my boy," said the Colonel, after a few more questions. "You run away home now. I expect it was some person trying to give you a start. Another time, like a brave English boy, you just throw a stone – well, no, not that exactly, but you go and speak to the waiter, or to Mr. Simpson, the landlord, and – yes – and say that I advised you to do so."

The boy's face expressed some of the doubt He felt as to the likelihood of Mr. Simpson's lending a favourable ear to his complaint, but the Colonel did not appear to perceive this, and went on :

"And here's a sixpence – no, I see it's a shilling – and you be off home, and don't think any more about it."

The youth hurried off with agitated thanks, and the Colonel and Parkins went round to the front of the Globe and reconnoitred. There was only one window answering to the description they had been hearing.

"Well, that's curious," said Parkins; "it's evidently my window the lad was talking about. Will you come up for a moment, Colonel Wilson? We ought to be able to see if anyone has been taking liberties in my room."

They were soon in the passage, and Parkins made as if to open the door. Then he stopped and felt in his pockets.

"This is more serious than I thought," was his next remark. "I remember now that before I started this morning I locked the door. It is locked now, and, what is more, here is the key." And he held it up. "Now," he went on, "if the servants are in the habit of going into one's room during the day when one is away, I can only say that – well, that I don't approve of it at all." Conscious of a somewhat weak climax, he busied himself in opening the door (which was indeed locked) and in lighting candles. "No," he said, "nothing seems disturbed."

"Except your bed," put in the Colonel.

"Excuse me, that isn't my bed," said Parkins. "I don't

use that one. But it does look as if someone had been playing tricks with it."

It certainly did : the clothes were bundled up and twisted together in a most tortuous confusion. Parkins pondered.

"That must be it," he said at last : "I disordered the clothes last night in unpacking, and they haven't made it since. Perhaps they came in to make it, and that boy saw them through the window; and then they were called away and locked the door after them. Yes, I think that must be it."

"Well, ring and ask," said the Colonel, and this appealed to Parkins as practical.

The maid appeared, and, to make a long story short, deposed that she had made the bed in the morning when the gentleman was in the room, and hadn't been there since. No, she hadn't no other key. Mr. Simpson he kep' the keys; he'd be able to tell the gentleman if anyone had been up.

This was a puzzle. Investigation showed that nothing of value had been taken, and Parkins remembered the disposition of the small objects on tables and so forth well enough to be pretty sure that no pranks had been played with them. Mr. and Mrs. Simpson furthermore agreed that neither of them had given the duplicate key of the room to any person whatever during the day. Nor could Parkins, fairminded man as he was, detect anything in the demeanour of master, mistress, or maid that indicated guilt. He was much more inclined to think that the boy had been imposing on the Colonel.

The latter was unwontedly silent and pensive at dinner and throughout the evening. When he bade good night to Parkins, he murmured in a gruff undertone :

"You know where I am if you want me during the night."

"Why, yes, thank you, Colonel Wilson, I think I do; but there isn't much prospect of my disturbing you, I hope. By the way," he added, "did I show you that old whistle I spoke of? I think not. Well, here it is."

The Colonel turned it over gingerly in the light of the candle.

"Can you make anything of the inscription?" asked Parkins, as he took it back.

"No, not in this light. What do you mean to do with it?"

"Oh, well, when I get back to Cambridge I shall submit it to some of the archæologists there, and see what they think of it; and very likely, if they consider it worth having, I may present it to one of the museums."

"'M!" said the Colonel. "Well, you may be right. All I know is that, if it were mine, I should chuck it straight into the sea. It's no use talking, I'm well aware, but I expect that with you it's a case of live and learn. I hope so, I'm sure, and I wish you a good night."

He turned away, leaving Parkins in act to speak at the bottom of the stair, and soon each was in his own bedroom.

By some unfortunate accident, there were neither blinds nor curtains to the windows of the Professor's room. The previous night he had thought little of this, but tonight there seemed every prospect of a bright moon rising to shine directly on his bed, and probably wake him later on. When he noticed this he was a good deal annoyed, but, with an ingenuity which I can only envy, he succeeded in rigging up, with the help of a railway-rug, some safety-pins, and a stick and umbrella, a screen which, if it only held together, would completely keep the moonlight off his bed. And shortly afterwards he was comfortably in that bed. When he had read a somewhat solid work long enough to produce a decided wish for sleep, he cast a drowsy glance round the room, blew out the candle, and fell back upon the pillow.

He must have slept soundly for an hour or more, when a sudden clatter shook him up in a most unwelcome manner. In a moment he realized what had happened : his carefully-constructed screen had given way, and a very bright frosty moon was shining directly on his face. This was highly annoying. Could he possibly get up and reconstruct the screen? or could he manage to sleep if he did not?

For some minutes he lay and pondered over the possibilities; then he turned over sharply, and with all his eyes open lay breathlessly listening. There had been a movement, he was sure, in the empty bed on the opposite side of the room. Tomorrow he would have it moved, for there must be rats or something playing about in it. It was quiet now. No! the commotion began again. There was a rustling and shaking : surely more than any rat could cause.

I can figure to myself something of the Professor's bewilderment and horror, for I have in a dream thirty years back seen the same thing happen; but the reader will hardly, perhaps, imagine how dreadful it was to him to see a figure suddenly sit up in what he had known was an empty bed. He was out of his own bed in one bound, and made a dash towards the window, where lay his only weapon, the stick with which he had propped his screen. This was, as it turned out, the worst thing he could have done, because the personage in the empty bed, with a sudden smooth motion, slipped from the bed and took up a position, with outspread arms, between the two beds, and in front of the door. Parkins watched it in a horrid perplexity. Somehow, the idea of getting past it and escaping through the door was intolerable to him; he could not have borne – he didn't know why – to touch it; and as for its touching him, he would sooner dash himself through the window than have that happen. It stood for the moment in a band of dark shadow, and he had not seen what its face was like. Now it began to move, in a stooping posture, and all at once the spectator realized, with some horror and some relief, that it must be blind, for it seemed to feel about it with its muffled arms in a groping and random fashion. Turning half away from him, it became suddenly conscious of the bed he had just left, and darted towards it, and bent over and felt the pillows in a way which made Parkins shudder as he had never in his life thought it possible. In a very few moments it seemed to know that the bed was empty, and then, moving forward into the area of light and facing the window, it showed for the first time what manner of thing it was.

Parkins, who very much dislikes being questioned about it, did once describe something of it in my hearing, and I gathered that what he chiefly remembers about it is a horrible, an intensely horrible, face *of crumpled linen.* What expression he read upon it he could not or would not tell, but that the fear of it went nigh to maddening him is certain.

But he was not at leisure to watch it for long. With formidable quickness it moved into the middle of the room, and, as it groped and waved, one corner of its draperies swept across Parkins's face. He could not – though he knew how perilous a sound was – he could not keep back a cry of disgust, and this gave the searcher an instant clue. It leapt towards him upon the instant, and the next moment he was half-way through the window backwards, uttering cry upon cry at the utmost pitch of his voice, and the linen face was thrust close into his own. At this, almost the last possible second, deliverance came, as you will have guessed : the Colonel burst the door open, and was just in time to see the dreadful group at the window. When he reached the figures only one was left. Parkins sank forward into the room in a faint, and before him on the floor lay a tumbled heap of bedclothes.

Colonel Wilson asked no questions, but busied himself in keeping everyone else out of the room and in getting Parkins back to his bed; and himself, wrapped in a rug, occupied the other bed for the rest of the night. Early on the next day Rogers arrived, more welcome than he would have been a day before, and the three of them held a very long consultation in the Professor's room. At the end of it the Colonel left the hotel door carrying a small object between his finger and thumb, which he cast as far into the sea as a very brawny arm could send it. Later on the smoke of a burning ascended from the back premises of the Globe.

Exactly what explanation was patched up for the staff and visitors at the hotel I must confess I do not recollect. The Professor was somehow cleared of the ready suspicion of delirium tremens, and the hotel of the reputation of a troubled house.

There is not much question as to what would have happened to Parkins if the Colonel had not intervened when he did. He would either have fallen out of the window or else lost his wits. But it is not so evident what more the creature that came in answer to the whistle could have done than frighten. There seemed to be absolutely nothing material about it save the bedclothes of which it had made itself a body. The Colonel, who remembered a not very dissimilar occurrence in India, was of opinion that if Parkins had closed with it it could really have done very little, and that its one power was that of frightening. The whole thing, he said, served to confirm his opinion of the Church of Rome.

There is really nothing more to tell, but, as you may imagine, the Professor's views on certain points are less clear cut than they used to be. His nerves, too, have suffered : he cannot even now see a surplice hanging on a door quite unmoved, and the spectacle of a scarecrow in a field late on a winter afternoon has cost him more than one sleepless night.

The Haunted Doll's House

'I suppose you get stuff of that kind through your
hands pretty often?' said Mr Dillet, as he pointed with
his stick to an object which shall be described when the
time comes: and when he said it, he lied in his throat,
and knew that he lied. Not once in twenty years – perhaps not once in a lifetime – could Mr Chittenden,
skilled as he was in ferreting out the forgotten
treasures of half-a-dozen counties, expect to handle
such a specimen. It was collectors' palaver, and Mr
Chittenden recognized it as such.

'Stuff of that kind, Mr Dillet! It's a museum piece,
that is.'

'Well, I suppose there are museums that'll take anything.'

'I've seen one, not as good as that, years back,' said Mr Chittenden, thoughtfully. 'But that's not likely to come into the market: and I'm told they 'ave some fine ones of the period over the water. No: I'm only telling you the truth, Mr Dillet, when I say that if you was to place an unlimited order with me for the very best that could be got – and you know I 'ave facilities for getting to know of such things, and a reputation to maintain – well, all I can say is, I should lead you straight up to that one and say, "I can't do no better for you than that, Sir."'

'Hear, hear!' said Mr Dillet, applauding ironically with the end of his stick on the floor of the shop. 'How much are you sticking the innocent American buyer for it, eh?'

'Oh, I shan't be over hard on the buyer, American or otherwise. You see, it stands this way, Mr Dillet – if I knew just a bit more about the pedigree –'

'Or just a bit less,' Mr Dillet put in.

'Ha, ha! you will have your joke, Sir. No, but as I was saying, if I knew just a little more than what I do about the piece – though anyone can see for themselves it's a genuine thing, every last corner of it, and there's not been one of my men allowed to so much as touch it since it came into the shop – there'd be another figure in the price I'm asking.'

'And what's that: five and twenty?'

'Multiply that by three and you've got it, Sir. Seventy-five's my price.'

'And fifty's mine,' said Mr Dillet.

The point of agreement was, of course, somewhere between the two, it does not matter exactly where – I think sixty guineas. But half an hour later the object was being packed, and within an hour Mr Dillet had called for it in his car and driven away. Mr Chittenden, holding the cheque in his hand, saw him off from the door with smiles, and returned, still smiling, into the parlour where his wife was making the tea. He stopped at the door.

'It's gone,' he said.

'Thank God for that!' said Mrs Chittenden, putting down the teapot. 'Mr Dillet, was it?'

'Yes, it was.'

'Well, I'd sooner it was him than another.'

'Oh, I don't know, he ain't a bad feller, my dear.'

'May be not, but in my opinion he'd be none the worse for a bit of a shake up.'

'Well, if that's your opinion, it's my opinion he's put himself into the way of getting one. Anyhow, we shan't have no more of it, and that's something to be thankful for.'

And so Mr and Mrs Chittenden sat down to tea.

And what of Mr Dillet and of his new acquisition? What it was, the title of this story will have told you. What it was like, I shall have to indicate as well as I can.

There was only just room enough for it in the car, and Mr Dillet had to sit with the driver: he had also to go slow, for though the rooms of the Doll's House had all been stuffed carefully with soft cotton-wool, jolting was to be avoided, in view of the immense number of small objects which thronged them; and the ten-mile drive was an anxious time for him, in spite of all the precautions he insisted upon. At last his front door was reached, and Collins, the butler, came out.

'Look here, Collins, you must help me with this

thing – it's a delicate job. We must get it out upright, see? It's full of little things that mustn't be displaced more than we can help. Let's see, where shall we have it? (After a pause for consideration.) Really, I think I shall have to put it in my own room, to begin with at any rate. On the big table – that's it.'

It was conveyed – with much talking – to Mr Dillet's spacious room on the first floor, looking out on the drive. The sheeting was unwound from it, and the front thrown open, and for the next hour or two Mr Dillet was fully occupied in extracting the padding and setting in order the contents of the rooms.

When this thoroughly congenial task was finished, I must say that it would have been difficult to find a more perfect and attractive specimen of a Doll's House in Strawberry Hill Gothic than that which now stood on Mr Dillet's large kneehole table, lighted up by the evening sun which came slanting through three tall sash-windows.

It was quite six feet long, including the Chapel or Oratory which flanked the front on the left as you faced it, and the stable on the right. The main block of the house was, as I have said, in the Gothic manner; that is to say, the windows had pointed arches and were surmounted by what are called ogival hoods, with crockets and finials such as we see on the canopies of tombs built into church walls. At the angles were absurd turrets covered with arched panels. The Chapel had pinnacles and buttresses and a bell in the turret and coloured glass in the windows. When the front of the house was open you saw four large rooms, bedroom, dining-room, drawing-room and kitchen, each with its appropriate furniture in a very complete state.

The stable on the right was in two storeys, with

its proper complement of horses, coaches and grooms, and with its clock and Gothic cupola for the clock bell.

Pages, of course, might be written on the outfit of the mansion—how many frying pans, how many gilt chairs, what pictures, carpets, chandeliers, four-posters, table linen, glass, crockery and plate it possessed; but all this must be left to the imagination. I will only say that the base or plinth on which the house stood (for it was fitted with one of some depth which allowed of a flight of steps to the front door and a terrace, partly balustraded) contained a shallow drawer or drawers in which were neatly stored sets of embroidered curtains, changes of raiment for the inmates, and, in short, all the materials for an infinite series of variations and refittings of the most absorbing and delightful kind.

'Quintessence of Horace Walpole, that's what it is: he must have had something to do with the making of it.' Such was Mr Dillet's murmured reflection as he knelt before it in a reverent ectasy. 'Simply wonderful; this is my day and no mistake. Five hundred pound coming in this morning for that cabinet which I never cared about, and now this tumbling into my hands for a tenth, at the very most, of what it would fetch in town. Well, well! It almost makes one afraid something'll happen to counter it. Let's have a look at the population, anyhow.'

Accordingly, he set them before him in a row. Again, here is an opportunity, which some would snatch at, of making an inventory of costume: I am incapable of it.

There were a gentleman and lady, in blue satin and brocade respectively. There were two children, a boy and a girl. There was a cook, a nurse, a footman, and there were the stable servants, two postillions, a coach-man, two grooms.

'Anyone else? Yes, possibly.'

The curtains of the four-poster in the bedroom were closely drawn round four sides of it, and he put his finger in between them and felt in the bed. He drew the finger back hastily, for it almost semed to him as if something had – not stirred, perhaps, but yielded – in an odd live way as he pressed it. Then he put back the curtains, which ran on rods in the proper manner, and extracted from the bed a white-haired old gentleman in a long linen nightdress and cap, and laid him down by the rest. The tale was complete.

Dinner time was now near, so Mr Dillet spent but five minutes in putting the lady and children into the drawing-room, the gentleman into the dining-room, the servants into the kitchen and stables, and the old man back into his bed. He retired into his dressing-room next door, and we see and hear no more of him until something like eleven o'clock at night.

His whim was to sleep surrounded by some of the gems of his collection. The big room in which we have seen him contained his bed: bath, wardrobe, and all the appliances of dressing were in a commodious room adjoining: but his four-poster, which itself was a valued treasure, stood in the large room where he sometimes wrote, and often sat, and even received visitors. To-night he repaired to it in a highly complacent frame of mind.

There was no striking clock within earshot – none on the staircase, none in the stable, none in the distant church tower. Yet it is indubitable that Mr Dillet was startled out of a very pleasant slumber by a bell tolling One.

He was so much startled that he did not merely lie breathless with wide-open eyes, but actually sat up in his bed.

He never asked himself, till the morning hours, how it was that, though there was no light at all in the room, the Doll's House on the kneehole table stood out with complete clearness. But it was so. The effect was that of a bright harvest moon shining full on the front of a big white stone mansion – a quarter of a mile away it might be, and yet every detail was photographically sharp. There were trees about it, too – trees rising behind the chapel and the house. He seemed to be conscious of the scent of a cool still September night. He thought he could hear an occasional stamp and clink from the stables, as of horses stirring. And with another shock he realized that, above the house, he was looking, not at the wall of his room with its pictures, but into the profound blue of a night sky.

There were lights, more than one, in the windows, and he quickly saw that this was no four-roomed house with a movable front, but one of many rooms, and staircases – a real house, but seen as if through the wrong end of a telescope. 'You mean to show me something,' he muttered to himself, and he gazed earnestly on the lighted windows. They would in real life have been shuttered or curtained, no doubt, he thought; but, as it was, there was nothing to intercept his view of what was being transacted inside the rooms.

Two rooms were lighted – one on the ground floor to the right of the door, one upstairs, on the left – the first brightly enough, the other rather dimly. The lower room was the dining-room: a table was laid, but the meal was over, and only wine and glasses were left on the table. The man of the blue satin and the woman of the brocade were alone in the room, and they were talking very earnestly, seated close together at the table, their elbows on it: every now and again stopping to listen, as it seemed. Once *he* rose, came to the window and opened it and put his head out and his hand to his ear. There was a lighted taper in a silver candlestick on a sideboard. When the man left the window he seemed to leave the room also; and the lady, taper in hand, remained standing and listening. The expression on her face was that of one striving her utmost to keep down a fear that threatened to master her – and succeeding. It was a hateful face, too; broad, flat and sly. Now the man came back and she took some small thing from him and hurried out of the room. He, too, disappeared, but only for a moment or two. The front door slowly opened and he stepped out and stood on the top of the *perron*, looking this way and that; then turned towards the upper window that was lighted, and shook his fist.

It was time to look at that upper window. Through it was seen a four-post bed: a nurse or other servant in an armchair, evidently sound asleep; in the bed an old man lying: awake, and, one would say, anxious, from the way in which he shifted about and moved his fingers, beating tunes on the coverlet. Beyond the bed a door opened. Light was seen on the ceiling, and the lady came in: she set down her candle on a table, came to the fireside and roused the nurse. In her hand she had an old-fashioned wine bottle, ready uncorked. The nurse took it, poured some of the contents into a little silver saucepan, added some spice and sugar from casters on the table, and set it to warm on the fire. Meanwhile the old man in the bed beckoned feebly to the feel his pulse, and bit her lip as if in consternation. He looked at her anxiously, and then pointed to the window, and spoke. She nodded, and did as the man below had done; opened the casement and listened – perhaps rather ostentatiously: then drew in her head and shook it, looking at the old man, who seemed to sigh.

By this time the posset on the fire was steaming, and the nurse poured it into a small two-handled silver bowl and brought it to the bedside. The old man seemed disinclined for it and was waving it away, but the lady and the nurse together bent over him and evidently pressed it upon him. He must have yielded, for they supported him into a sitting position, and put it to his lips. He drank most of it, in several draughts, and they laid him down. The lady left the room, smiling goodnight to him, and took the bowl, the bottle and the silver saucepan with her. The nurse returned to the chair, and there was an interval of complete quiet.

Suddenly the old man started up in his bed – and he must have uttered some cry, for the nurse started out of her chair and made but one step of it to the bedside. He was a sad and terrible sight – flushed in the face, almost to blackness, the eyes glaring whitely, both hands clutching at his heart, foam at his lips.

For a moment the nurse left him, ran to the door, flung it wide open, and, one supposes, screamed aloud for help, then darted back to the bed and seemed to try feverishly to soothe him – to lay him down – anything. But as the lady, her husband, and several servants, rushed into the room with horrified faces, the old man collapsed under the nurse's hands and lay back, and the features, contorted with agony and rage, relaxed slowly into calm.

A few moments later, lights showed out to the left of

the house, and a coach with flambeaux drove up to the door. A white-wigged man in black got nimbly out and ran up the steps, carrying a small leather trunk-shaped box. He was met in the doorway by the man and his wife, she with her handkerchief clutched between her hands, he with a tragic face, but retaining his self-control. They led the newcomer into the dining-room, where he set his box of papers on the table, and, turning to them, listened with a face of consternation at what they had to tell. He nodded his head again and again, threw out his hands slightly, declined, it seemed, offers of refreshment and lodging for the night, and within a few minutes came slowly down the steps, entering the coach and driving off the way he had come. As the man in blue watched him from the top of the steps, a smile not pleasant to see stole slowly over his fat white face. Darkness fell over the whole scene as the lights of the coach disappeared.

But Mr Dillet remained sitting up in the bed: he had rightly guessed that there would be a sequel. The house front glimmered out again before long. But now there was a difference. The lights were in other windows, one at the top of the house, the other illuminating the range of coloured windows of the chapel. How he saw through these is not quite obvious, but he did. The interior was as carefully furnished as the rest of the establishment, with its minute red cushions on the desks, its Gothic stall-canopies, and its western gallery and pinnacled organ with gold pipes. On the centre of the black and white pavement was a bier: four tall candles burned at the corners. On the bier was a coffin covered with a pall of black velvet.

As he looked the folds of the pall stirred. It seemed to rise at one end: it slid downwards: it fell away, exposing the black coffin with its silver handles and name-plate. One of the tall candlesticks swayed and toppled over. Ask no more, but turn, as Mr Dillet hastily did, and look in at the lighted window at the top of the house, where a boy and girl lay in two truckle-beds, and a four-poster for the nurse rose above them. The nurse was not visible for the moment; but the father and mother were there, dressed now in mourning, but with very little sign of mourning in their demeanour. Indeed, they were laughing and talking with a good deal of animation, sometimes to each other, and sometimes throwing a remark to one or other of the children, and again laughing at the answers. Then the father was seen to go on tiptoe out of the room, taking with him as he went a white garment that hung on a peg near the door. He shut the door after him. A minute or two later it was slowly opened again, and a muffled head poked round it. A bent form of sinister shape stepped across to the truckle-beds, and suddenly stopped, threw up its arms and revealed, of course, the father, laughing. The children were in agonies of terror, the boy with the bedclothes over his head, the girl throwing herself out of bed into her mother's arms. Attempts at consolation followed – the parents took the children on their laps, patted them, picked up the white gown and showed there was no harm in it, and so forth; and at last putting the children back into bed, left the room with encouraging waves of the hand. As they left it, the nurse came in, and soon the light died down.

Still Mr Dillet watched immovable.

A new sort of light – not of lamp or candle – a pale ugly light, began to dawn around the door-case at the back of the room. The door was opening again. The seer does not like to dwell upon what he saw entering the room: he says it might be described as a frog – the size of a man – but it had scanty white hair about its head. It was busy about the truckle-beds, but not for long. The sound of cries – faint, as if coming out of a vast distance – but, even so, infinitely appalling, reached the ear.

There were signs of a hideous commotion all over the house: lights passed along and up, and doors opened and shut, and running figures passed within the windows. The clock in the stable turret tolled one, and darkness fell again.

It was only dispelled once more, to show the house front. At the bottom of the steps dark figures were drawn up in two lines, holding flaming torches. More dark figures came down the steps, bearing, first one, then another small coffin. And the lines of torch-bearers with the coffins between them moved silently onward to the left.

The hours of night passed on – never so slowly, Mr Dillet thought. Gradually he sank down from sitting to lying in his bed – but he did not close an eye: and early next morning he sent for the doctor.

The doctor found him in a disquieting state of nerves, and recommended sea air. To a quiet place on the East Coast he accordingly repaired by easy stages in his car.

One of the first people he met on the sea front was Mr Chittenden, who, it appeared, had likewise been advised to take his wife away for a bit of a change.

Mr Chittenden looked somewhat askance upon him when they met: and not without cause.

'Well, I don't wonder at you being a bit upset, Mr Dillet. What? Yes, well, I might say 'orrible upset, to be sure, seeing what me and my poor wife went through ourselves. But I put it to you, Mr Dillet, one of two things: was I going to scrap a lovely piece like that on the one 'and, or was I going to tell customers: "I'm selling you a regular picture-palace-dramar in reel life of the olden time, billed to perform regular at one o'clock a.m."? Why, what would you 'ave said yourself? And next thing you know, two Justices of the Peace in the back parlour, and pore Mr and Mrs Chittenden off in a spring cart to the County Asylum and everyone in the street saying, "Ah, I thought it 'ud come to that. Look at the way the man drank!" – and me next door, or next door but one, to a total abstainer, as you know. Well, there was my position. What? Me 'ave it back in the shop? Well, what do *you* think? No, but I'll tell you what I will do. You shall have your money back, bar the ten pound I paid for it, and you make what you can.'

Later in the day, in what is offensively called the 'smoke-room' of the hotel, a murmured conversation between the two went on for some time.

'How much do you really know about that thing, and where it came from?'

'Honest, Mr Dillet, I don't know the 'ouse. Of course, it came out of the lumber room of a country 'ouse – that anyone could guess. But I'll go as far as say this, that I believe it's not a hundred miles from this place. Which direction and how far I've no notion. I'm only judging by guesswork. The man as I actually paid the cheque to ain't one of my regular men, and I've lost sight of him; but I 'ave the idea that this part of the country was his beat, and that's every word I can tell you. But now, Mr Dillet, there's one thing that rather physics me – that old chap – I suppose you saw him drive up to the door – I thought so: now, would he have been the medical man, do you take it? My wife would have it so, but I stuck to it that was the lawyer, because he had papers·with him, and one he took out was folded up.'

'I agree,' said Mr Dillet. 'Thinking it over, I came to the conclusion that was the old man's will, ready to be signed.'

'Just what I thought,' said Mr Chittenden, 'and I took ĩt that will would have cut out the young people, eh? Well, well! It's been a lesson to me, I know that. I shan't buy no more dolls' houses, nor waste no more money on the pictures – and as to this business of poisonin' grandpa, well, if I know myself, I never 'ad much of a turn for that. Live and let live: that's bin my motto throughout life, and I ain't found it a bad one.'

Filled with these elevated sentiments, Mr Chittenden retired to his lodgings. Mr Dillet next day repaired to the local institute, where he hoped to find some clue to the riddle that absorbed him. He gazed in despair at a long file of the Canterbury and York Society's publications of the Parish Registers of the district. No print resembling the house of his nightmare was among those that hung on the staircase and in the passages. Disconsolate, he found himself at last in a derelict room, staring at a dusty model of a church in a dusty glass case: *Model of St Stephen's Church, Coxham. Presented by J. Merewether, Esq., of Ilbridge House, 1877. The work of his ancestor James Merewether, d. 1786.* There was something in the fashion of it that reminded him dimly of his horror. He retraced his steps to a wall map he had noticed, and made out that Ilbridge House was in Coxham Parish. Coxham was, as it happened, one of the parishes of which he had retained the name when he glanced over the file of printed registers, and it was not long before he found in them the record of the burial of Roger Milford, aged 76, on the 11th of September, 1757, and of Roger and Elizabeth Merewether, aged 9 and 7, on the 19th of the same month. It seemed worthwhile to follow up this clue, frail as it was; and in the afternoon he drove out to Coxham. The east end of the north aisle of the church is a Milford chapel, and on its north wall are tablets to the same persons; Roger, the elder, it seems, was distinguished by all the qualities which adorn 'the Father, the Magistrate, and the Man': the memorial was erected by his detached daughter Elizabeth, 'who did not long survive the loss of a parent ever solicitous for her welfare, and of two amiable children'. The last sentence was plainly an addition to the original inscription.

A yet later slab told of James Merewether, husband of Elizabeth, 'who in the dawn of life practised, not without success, those arts which, had he continued their exercise, might in the opinion of the most competent judges have earned for him the name of the British Vitruvius: but who, overwhelmed by the visitation which deprived him of an affectionate partner and a blooming offspring, passed his Prime and Age in a secluded yet elegant Retirement: his grateful Nephew and Heir indulges a pious sorrow by this too brief recital of his excellences.'

The children were more simply commemorated. Both died on the night of the 12th of September.

Mr Dillet felt sure that in Ilbridge House he had found the scene of his drama. In some old sketch book, possibly in some old print, he may yet find convincing evidence that he is right. But the Ilbridge House of today is not that which he sought; it is an Elizabethan erection of the forties, in red brick with stone quoins and dressings. A quarter of a mile from it, in a low part of the park, backed by ancient, stag-horned, ivy-strangled trees and thick undergrowth, are marks of a terraced platform overgrown with rough grass. A few stone balusters lie here and there, and a heap or two, covered with nettles and ivy, of wrought stones with badly carved crockets. This, someone told Mr Dillet, was the site of an older house.

As he drove out of the village, the hall clock struck four, and Mr Dillet started up and clapped his hands to his ears. It was not the first time he had heard that bell.

Awaiting an offer from the other side of the Atlantic, the doll's house still reposes, carefully sheeted, in a loft over Mr Dillet's stables, whither Collins conveyed it on the day when Mr Dillet started for the sea coast.

THE MALICE OF INANIMATE
OBJECTS

The malice of inanimate objects is a subject upon which an old
friend of mine was fond of dilating, and not without justifica-
tion. In the lives of all of us, short or long, there have been

days, dreadful days, on which we have had to acknowledge with gloomy resignation that our world has turned against us. I do not mean the human world of our relations and friends: to enlarge on that is the province of nearly every modern novelist. In their books it is called 'Life' and an odd enough hash it is as they portray it. No, it is the world of things that do not speak or work or hold congresses and conferences. It includes such beings as the collar stud, the inkstand, the fire, the razor, and, as age increases, the extra step on the staircase which leads you either to expect or not to expect it. By these and such as these (for I have named but the merest fraction of them) the word is passed round, and the day of misery arranged.

Is the tale still remembered of how the Cock and the Hen went to pay a visit to Squire Korbes? How on the journey they met with and picked up a number of associates, encouraging each with the announcement:

> 'To Squire Korbes we are going
> For a visit is owing.'

Thus they secured the company of the Needle, the Egg, the Duck, the Cat, possibly – for memory is a little treacherous here – and finally the Millstone: and when it was discovered that Squire Korbes was for the moment out, they took up positions in his mansion and awaited his return. He did return, wearied no doubt by a day's work among his extensive properties. His nerves were first jarred by the raucous cry of the Cock. He threw himself into his armchair and was lacerated by the Needle. He went to the sink for a refreshing wash and was splashed all over by the Duck. Attempting to dry himself with the towel he broke the Egg upon his face. He suffered other indignities from the Hen and her accomplices, which I cannot now recollect, and finally, maddened with pain and fear, rushed out by the back door and had his brains dashed out by the Millstone that had perched itself in the appropriate place. 'Truly,' in the concluding words of the story, 'this Squire Korbes must have been either a very wicked or a very unfortunate man.' It is the latter alternative which I incline to accept. There is nothing in the preliminaries to show that any slur rested on his name, or that his visitors had any injury to avenge. And will not this narrative serve as a striking example of that malice of which I have taken upon me to treat? It is, I know, the fact that Squire Korbes's visitors were not all of them, strictly speaking, inanimate. But are we sure that the perpetrators of this malice are really inanimate either? There are tales which seem to justify a doubt.

Two men of mature years were seated in a pleasant garden after breakfast. One was reading the day's paper, the other sat with folded arms, plunged in thought, and on his face were a piece of sticking plaster and lines of care. His companion lowered his paper. 'What,' said he, 'is the matter with you? The morning is bright, the birds are singing, I can hear no aeroplanes or motor bikes.'

'No,' replied Mr Burton, 'It is nice enough, I agree, but I have a bad day before me. I cut myself shaving and spilt my tooth powder.'

'Ah,' said Mr Manners, 'some people have all the luck,' and with this expression of sympathy he reverted to his paper. 'Hullo,' he exclaimed, after a moment, 'here's George Wilkins dead! You won't have any more bother with him, anyhow.'

'George Wilkins?' said Mr Burton, more than a little excitedly. 'Why, I didn't even know he was ill.'

'No more he was, poor chap. Seems to have thrown up the sponge and put an end to himself. Yes,' he went on, 'it's some days back: this is the inquest. Seemed very much worried and depressed, they say. What about, I wonder? Could it have been that will you and he were having a row about?'

'Row?' said Mr Burton angrily. 'There was no row: he hadn't a leg to stand on: he couldn't bring a scrap of evidence. No, it may have been half-a-dozen things: but Lord! I never imagined he'd take anything so hard as that.'

'I don't know,' said Mr Manners, 'he was a man, I thought, who did take things hard: they rankled. Well, I'm sorry, though I never saw much of him. He must have gone through a lot to make him cut his throat. Not the way I should choose, by a long sight. Ugh! Lucky he hadn't a family, anyhow. Look here, what about a walk round before lunch? I've an errand in the village.'

Mr Burton assented rather heavily. He was perhaps reluctant to give the inanimate objects of the district a chance of getting at him. If so, he was right. He just escaped a nasty purl over the scraper at the top of the steps: a thorny branch swept off his hat and scratched his fingers, and as they climbed a grassy slope he fairly leapt into the air with a cry and came down flat on his face.

'What in the world?' said his friend coming up. 'A great string, of all things! What business – oh, I see – belongs to that kite' (which lay on the grass a little farther up). 'Now if I can find out what little beast has left that kicking about, I'll let him have it – or rather I won't, for he shan't see his kite again. It's rather a good one, too.'

As they approached, a puff of wind raised the kite and it seemed to sit up on its end and look at them with two large round eyes painted red, and, below them, three large printed red letters: ICU.

Mr Manners was amused and scanned the device with care. 'Ingenious,' he said. 'It's a bit off a poster, of course: I see! "FULL PARTICULARS", the word was.'

Mr Burton on the other hand was not amused, but thrust his stick through the kite. Mr Manners was inclined to regret this. 'I dare say it serves him right,' he said, 'but he'd taken a lot of trouble to make it.'

'Who had?' said Mr Burton sharply. 'Oh, I see, you mean the boy.'

'Yes, to be sure, who else? But come on down now: I want to leave a message before lunch.'

As they turned a corner into the main street, a rather muffled and choky voice was heard to say 'Look out! I'm coming.' They both stopped as if they had been shot.

'Who *was* that?' said Manners. 'Blest if I didn't think I knew' – then, with almost a yell of laughter he pointed with his stick. A cage with a grey parrot in it was hanging in an open window across the way. 'I *was* startled, by George: it gave you a bit of a turn, too, didn't it?' Burton was inaudible. 'Well, I shan't be a minute: you can go and make friends with the bird.'

But when he rejoined Burton, that unfortunate was not, it seemed, in trim for talking with either birds or men; he was some way ahead and going rather quickly. Manners paused for an instant at the parrot window and then hurried on laughing more than ever. 'Have a good talk with Polly?' said he, as he came up.

'No, of course not,' said Burton, testily. 'I didn't bother about the beastly thing.'

'Well, you wouldn't have got much out of her if you'd tried,' said Manners. 'I remembered after a bit; they've had her in the window for years: she's stuffed.' Burton seemed about to make a remark, but suppressed it.

Decidedly this was not Burton's day out. He choked at lunch, he broke a pipe, he tripped on the carpet, he dropped his book in the pond in the garden. Later on he had or professed to have a telephone call summoning him back to town next day and cutting short what should have been a week's visit. And so glum was he all evening that Manners' disappointment in losing an ordinarily cheerful companion was not very sharp.

At breakfast Mr Burton said little about his night: but he did intimate that he thought of looking in on his doctor. 'My hand's so shaky,' he said, 'I really daren't shave this morning.'

'Oh, I'm sorry,' said Mr Manners. 'My man could have managed that for you: but they'll put you right in no time.'

Farewells were said. By some means and for some reason Mr Burton contrived to reserve a compartment to himself. (The train was not of the corridor type.) But these precautions avail little against the angry dead.

I will not put dots or stars, for I dislike them, but I will say that apparently someone tried to shave Mr Burton in the train, and did not succeed overly well. He was however satisfied with what he had done, if we may judge from the fact that on a once white napkin spread on Mr Burton's chest was an inscription in red letters: GEO. W. FECI.

Do not these facts – if facts they are – bear out my suggestion that there is something not inanimate behind the malice of inanimate objects? Do they not further suggest that when this malice begins to show itself, we should be very particular to examine and, if possible, rectify any obliquities in our recent conduct? And do they not, finally, almost force upon us the conclusion that, like Squire Korbes, Mr Burton must have been either a very wicked or a singularly unfortunate man?

The Treasure of Abbot Thomas

I

'VERUM usque in præsentem diem multa garriunt inter se
Canonici de abscondito quodam istius Abbatis Thomæ
thesauro, quem sæpe, quanquam adhuc incassum quæsi-
verunt Steinfeldenses. Ipsum enim Thomam adhuc florida in
ætate existentem ingentem auri massam circa monasterium
defodisse perhibent; de quo multoties interrogatus ubi esset,
cum risu respondere solitus erat: "Job, Johannes, et
Zacharias vel vobis vel posteris indicabunt"; idemque
aliquando adiicere se inventuris minime invisurum. Inter alia
huius Abbatis opera, hoc memoria præcipue dignum iudico
quod fenestram magnam in orientali parte alæ australis in
ecclesia sua imaginibus optime in vitro depictis impleverit: id
quod et ipsius effigies et insignia ibidem posita demonstrant.
Domum quoque Abbatialem fere totam restauravit: puteo in
atrio ipsius effosso et lapidibus marmoreis pulchre cælatis

157

exornato. Decessit autem, morte aliquantulum subitanea perculsus, ætatis suæ anno lxxii^{do}, incarnationis vero Dominiæ mdxxix°.'

'I suppose I shall have to translate this,' said the antiquary to himself, as he finished copying the above lines from that rather rare and exceedingly diffuse book, the *'Sertum Steinfeldense Norbertinum.'*[*] 'Well, it may as well be done first as last,' and accordingly the following rendering was very quickly produced:

'Up to the present day there is much gossip among the Canons about a certain hidden treasure of this Abbot Thomas, for which those of Steinfeld have often made search, though hitherto in vain. The story is that Thomas, while yet in the vigour of life, concealed a very large quantity of gold somewhere in the monastery. He was often asked where it was, and always answered, with a laugh: "Job, John, and Zechariah will tell either you or your successors." He sometimes added that he should feel no grudge against those who might find it. Among other works carried out by this Abbot I may specially mention his filling the great window at the east end of the south aisle of the church with figures admirably painted on glass, as his effigy and arms in the window attest. He also restored almost the whole of the Abbot's lodging, and dug a well in the court of it, which he adorned with beautiful carvings in marble. He died rather suddenly in the seventy-second year of his age, AD 1529.'

The object which the antiquary had before him at the moment was that of tracing the whereabouts of the painted windows of the Abbey Church of Steinfeld. Shortly after the Revolution, a very large quantity of painted glass had made its way from the dissolved abbeys of Germany and Belgium to this country, and may now be seen adorning various of our parish churches, cathedrals, and private chapels. Steinfeld Abbey was among the most considerable of these involuntary contributors to our artistic possessions (I am quoting the somewhat ponderous preamble of the book which the

* An account of the Premonstratensian abbey of Steinfeld, in the Eiffel, with lives of the Abbots, published at Cologne in 1712 by Christian Albert Erhard, a resident in the district. The epithet *Norbertinum* is due to the fact that St Norbert was founder of the Premonstratensian Order.

antiquary wrote), and the greater part of the glass from that institution can be identified without much difficulty by the help, either of the numerous inscriptions in which the place is mentioned, or of the subjects of the windows, in which several well-defined cycles or narratives were represented.

The passage with which I began my story had set the antiquary on the track of another identification. In a private chapel – no matter where – he had seen three large figures, each occupying a whole light in a window, and evidently the work of one artist. Their style made it plain that that artist had been a German of the sixteenth century; but hitherto the more exact localizing of them had been a puzzle. They represented – will you be surprised to hear it? – JOB PATRIARCHA, JOHANNES EVANGELISTA, ZACHARIAS PROPHETA, and each of them held a book or scroll, inscribed with a sentence from his writings. These, as a matter of course, the antiquary had noted, and had been struck by the curious way in which they differed from any text of the Vulgate that he had been able to examine. Thus the scroll in Job's hand was inscribed: 'Auro est locus in quo absconditur' (for 'conflatur')*; on the book of John was: 'Habent in vestimentis suis scripturam quam nemo novit't (for 'in vestimento scriptum', the following words being taken from another verse); and Zacharias had: 'Super lapidem unum septem oculi sunt'‡ (which alone of the three presents an unaltered text).

A sad perplexity it had been to our investigator to think why these three personages should have been placed together in one window. There was no bond of connection between them, either historic, symbolic, or doctrinal, and he could only suppose that they must have formed part of a very large series of Prophets and Apostles, which might have filled, say, all the clerestory windows of some capacious church. But the passage from the 'Sertum' had altered the situation by showing that the names of the actual personages represented in the glass now in Lord D —'s chapel had been constantly on the lips of Abbot Thomas von Eschenhausen of Steinfeld, and

* There is a place for gold where it is hidden.
† They have on their raiment a writing which no man knoweth.
‡ Upon one stone are seven eyes.

that this Abbot had put up a painted widow, probably about the year 1520, in the south aisle of his abbey church. It was no very wild conjecture that the three figures might have formed part of Abbot Thomas's offering; it was one which, moreover, could probably be confirmed or set aside by another careful examination of the glass. And, as Mr Somerton was a man of leisure, he set out on pilgrimage to the private chapel with very little delay. His conjecture was confirmed to the full. Not only did the style and technique of the glass suit perfectly with the date and place required, but in another window of the chapel he found some glass, known to have been bought along with the figures, which contained the arms of Abbot Thomas von Eschenhausen.

At intervals during his researches Mr Somerton had been haunted by the recollection of the gossip about the hidden treasure, and, as he thought the matter over, it became more and more obvious to him that if the Abbot meant anything by the enigmatical answer which he gave to his questioners, he must have meant that the secret was to be found somewhere in the window he had placed in the abbey church. It was undeniable, furthermore, that the first of the curiously-selected texts on the scrolls in the window might be taken to have a reference to hidden treasure.

Every feature, therefore, or mark which could possibly assist in elucidating the riddle which, he felt sure, the Abbot had set to posterity he noted with scrupulous care, and, returning to his Berkshire manor-house, consumed many a pint of the midnight oil over his tracings and sketches. After two or three weeks, a day came when Mr Somerton announced to his man that he must pack his own and his master's things for a short journey abroad, whither for the moment we will not follow him.

II

Mr Gregory, the Rector of Parsbury, had strolled out before breakfast, it being a fine autumn morning, as far as the gate of his carriage-drive, with intent to meet the postman and sniff the cool air. Nor was he disappointed of either purpose. Before he had had time to answer more than ten or eleven of the miscellaneous questions propounded to him in the lightness of their hearts by his young offspring, who had accompanied him, the postman was seen approaching; and among the morning's budget was one letter bearing a foreign postmark and stamp (which became at once the object of an eager competition among the youthful Gregorys), and was addressed in an uneducated, but plainly an English hand.

When the Rector opened it, and turned to the signature, he realized that it came from the confidential valet of his friend and squire, Mr Somerton. Thus it ran:

'HONOURED SIR,

'Has I am in a great anxeity about Master I write at is Wish to Beg you Sir if you could be so good as Step over. Master Has add a Nastey Shock and keeps His Bedd. I never Have known Him like this but No wonder and Nothing will serve but you Sir. Master says would I mintion the Short Way Here is Drive to Cobblince and take a Trap. Hopeing I Have maid all Plain, but am much Confuse'd in Myself what with Anxiatey and Weakfulness at Night. If I might be so Bold Sir it will be a Pleasure to see a Honnest Brish Face among all These Forig ones.

'I am Sir
'Your obed' Serv'
'WILLIAM BROWN.

'P.S. – The Villiage for Town I will not Turm. It is name Steenfeld.'

The reader must be left to picture to himself in detail the surprise, confusion and hurry of preparation into which the receipt of such a letter would be likely to plunge a quiet Berkshire parsonage in the year of grace 1859. It is enough for me to say that a train to town was caught in the course of the day, and that Mr Gregory was able to secure a cabin in the Antwerp boat and a place in the Coblentz train. Nor was it difficult to manage the transit from that centre to Steinfeld.

I labour under a grave disadvantage as narrator of this story in that I have never visited Steinfeld myself, and that neither of the principal actors in the episode (from whom I derive my information) was able to give me anything but a vague and rather dismal idea of its appearance. I gather that it is a small place, with a large church despoiled of its ancient fittings; a number of rather ruinous great buildings, mostly of the seventeenth century, surround this church; for the abbey, in common with most of those on the Continent, was rebuilt in a luxurious fashion by its inhabitants at that period. It has not seemed to me worth while to lavish money on a visit to the place, for though it is probably far more attractive than either Mr Somerton or Mr Gregory thought it, there is evidently little, if anything, of first-rate interest to be seen – except, perhaps, one thing, which I should not care to see.

The inn where the English gentleman and his servant were lodged is, or was, the only 'possible' one in the village. Mr Gregory was taken to it at once by his driver, and found Mr Brown waiting at the door. Mr Brown, a model when in his Berkshire home of the impassive whiskered race who are known as confidential valets, was now egregiously out of his element, in a light tweed suit, anxious, almost irritable, and plainly anything but master of the situation. His relief at the sight of the 'honest British face' of his Rector was unmeasured, but words to describe it were denied him. He could only say:

'Well, I ham pleased, I'm sure, sir, to see you. And so I'm sure, sir, will master.'

'How *is* your master, Brown?' Mr Gregory eagerly put in.

'I think he's better, sir, thank you; but he's had a dreadful time of it. I 'ope he's gettin' some sleep now, but –'

'What has been the matter – I couldn't make out from your letter? Was it an accident of any kind?'

'Well, sir, I 'ardly know whether I'd better speak about it. Master was very partickler he should be the one to tell you. But there's no bones broke – that's one thing I'm sure we ought to be thankful –'

'What does the doctor say?' asked Mr Gregory.

They were by this time outside Mr Somerton's bedroom door, and speaking in low tones. Mr Gregory, who happened to be in front, was feeling for the handle, and chanced to run his fingers over the panels. Before Brown could answer, there was a terrible cry from within the room.

'In God's name, who is that?' were the first words they heard. 'Brown, is it?'

'Yes, sir – me, sir, and Mr Gregory,' Brown hastened to answer, and there was an audible groan of relief in reply.

They entered the room, which was darkened against the afternoon sun, and Mr Gregory saw, with a shock of pity, how drawn, how damp with drops of fear, was the usually calm face of his friend, who, sitting up in the curtained bed, stretched out a shaking hand to welcome him.

'Better for seeing you, my dear Gregory,' was the reply to the Rector's first question; and it was palpably true.

After five minutes of conversation Mr Somerton was more his own man, Brown afterwards reported, than he had been for days. He was able to eat a more than respectable dinner, and talked confidently of being fit to stand a journey to Coblentz within twenty-four hours.

'But there's one thing,' he said, with a return of agitation which Mr Gregory did not like to see, 'which I must beg you to do for me, my dear Gregory. Don't,' he went on, laying his hand on Gregory's to forestall any interruption – 'don't ask me what it is, or why I want it done. I'm not up to explaining it yet; it would throw me back – undo all the good you have done me by coming. The only word I will say about it is that you run no risk whatever by doing it, and that Brown can and will show you to-morrow what it is. It's merely to put back – to keep – something – No; I can't speak of it yet. Do you mind · calling Brown?'

'Well, Somerton,' said Mr Gregory, as he crossed the room to the door, 'I won't ask for any explanations till you see fit to give them. And if this bit of business is as easy as you represent it to be, I will very gladly undertake it for you the first thing in the morning.'

'Ah, I was sure you would, my dear Gregory; I was certain I could rely on you. I shall owe you more thanks than I can tell. Now, here is Brown. Brown, one word with you.'

'Shall I go?' interjected Mr Gregory.

'Not at all. Dear me, no. Brown, the first thing to-morrow morning – (you don't mind early hours, I know, Gregory) – you must take the Rector to – *there*, you know' (a nod from Brown, who looked grave and anxious), 'and he and you will put that back. You needn't be in the least alarmed; it's *perfectly* safe in the daytime. You know what I mean. It lies on the step, you know, where – where we put it.' (Brown swallowed dryly once or twice, and, failing to speak, bowed.) 'And – yes, that's all. Only this one other word, my dear Gregory. If you *can* manage to keep from questioning Brown about this matter, I shall be still more bound to you. To-morrow evening, at latest, if all goes well, I shall be able, I believe, to tell you the whole story from start to finish. And now I'll wish you good-night. Brown will be with me – he sleeps here – and if I were you, I should lock my door. Yes, be particular to do that. They – they like it, the people here, and it's better. Good-night, good-night.'

They parted upon this, and if Mr Gregory woke once or twice in the small hours and fancied he heard a fumbling about the lower part of his locked door, it was, perhaps, no more than what a quiet man, suddenly plunged into a strange bed and the heart of a mystery, might reasonably expect. Certainly he thought, to the end of his days, that he had heard such a sound twice or three times between midnight and dawn.

He was up with the sun, and out in company with Brown soon after. Perplexing as was the service he had been asked to perform for Mr Somerton, it was not a difficult or an alarming one, and within half an hour from his leaving the inn it was over. What it was I shall not as yet divulge.

Later in the morning Mr Somerton, now almost himself again, was able to make a start from Steinfeld; and that same evening, whether at Coblentz or at some intermediate stage on the journey I am not certain, he settled down to the promised explanation. Brown was present, but how much of the matter was ever really made plain to his comprehension he would never say, and I am unable to conjecture.

III

This was Mr Somerton's story:

'You know roughly, both of you, that this expedition of mine was undertaken with the object of tracing something in connection with some old painted glass in Lord D — 's private chapel. Well, the starting-point of the whole matter lies in this passage from an old printed book, to which I will ask your attention.'

And at this point Mr Somerton went carefully over some ground with which we are already familiar.

'On my second visit to the chapel,' he went on, 'my purpose was to take every note I could of figures, lettering, diamond-scratchings on the glass, and even apparently accidental markings. The first point which I tackled was that of the inscribed scrolls. I could not doubt that the first of these, that of Job – "There is a place for the gold where it is hidden" – with its intentional alteration, must refer to the treasure; so I applied myself with some confidence to the next, that of St John – "They have on their vestures a writing which no man knoweth." The natural question will have occurred to you: Was there an inscription on the robes of the figures? I could see none; each of the three had a broad black border to his mantle, which made a conspicuous and rather ugly feature in the window. I was nonplussed, I will own, and but for a curious bit of luck I think I should have left the search where the Canons of Steinfeld had left it before me. But it so happened that there was a good deal of dust on the surface of the glass, and Lord D —, happening to come in, noticed my blackened hands, and kindly insisted on sending for a Turk's head broom to clean down the window. There must, I suppose, have been a rough piece in the broom; anyhow, as it passed over the border of one of the mantles, I noticed that it left a long scratch, and that some yellow stain instantly showed up. I asked the man to stop his work for a moment, and ran up the ladder to examine the place. The yellow stain was there, sure enough, and what had come away was a thick black pigment, which had evidently been laid on with the brush after the glass had been burnt, and could therefore be easily scraped off without doing any harm. I scraped, accordingly, and you will hardly believe – no, I do you an injustice; you will have guessed already – that I found under this black pigment two or three clearly-formed capital letters in yellow stain on a clear ground. Of course, I could hardly contain my delight.

'I told Lord D — that I had detected an inscription which I thought might be very interesting, and begged to be allowed to uncover the whole of it. He made no difficulty about it whatever, told me to do exactly as I pleased, and then, having an engagement, was obliged – rather to my relief, I must say – to leave me. I set to work at once, and found the task a fairly easy one. The pigment, disintegrated, of course, by time, came off almost at a touch, and I don't think that it took me a couple of hours, all told, to clean the whole of the black borders in all three lights. Each of the figures had, as the inscription said, "a writing on their vestures which nobody knew".

'This discovery, of course, made it absolutely certain to my mind that I was on the right track. And, now, what was the inscription? While I was cleaning the glass I almost took pains not to read the lettering, saving up the treat until I had got the whole thing clear. And when that *was* done, my dear Gregory, I assure you I could almost have cried from sheer disappointment. What I read was only the most hopeless jumble of letters that was ever shaken up in a hat.

Here it is:

Job. DREVICIOPEDMOOMSMVIVLISLCAVIBASBATA-OVT

St. John. RDIIEAMRLESIPVSPODSEEIRSETTAAESGIAV-NNR

Zechariah. FTEEAILNQDPVAIVMTLEEATTOHIOONV-MCAAT. H.Q.E.

'Blank as I felt and must have looked for the first few minutes, my disappointment didn't last long. I realized almost at once that I was dealing with a cipher or cryptogram; and I reflected that it was likely to be of a pretty simple kind, considering its early date. So I copied the letters with the most anxious care. Another little point, I may tell you, turned up in the process which confirmed my belief in the cipher. After copying the letters on Job's robe I counted them, to make sure that I had them right. There were thirty-eight; and, just as I finished going through them, my eye fell on a scratching made with a sharp point on the edge of the border. It was simply the number xxxviii in Roman numerals. To cut the matter short, there was a similar note, as I may call it, in each of the other lights; and that made it plain to me that the glass-painter had had very strict orders from Abbot Thomas about the inscription, and had taken pains to get it correct.

'Well, after that discovery you may imagine how minutely I went over the whole surface of the glass in search of further light. Of course, I did not neglect the inscription on the scroll of Zechariah – "Upon one stone are seven eyes", but I very quickly concluded that this must refer to some mark on a stone which could only be found *in situ*, where the treasure was concealed. To be short, I made all possible notes and sketches and tracings, and then came back to Parsbury to work out the cipher at leisure. Oh, the agonies I went through! I thought myself very clever at first, for I made sure that the key would be found in some of the old books on secret writing. The "*Steganographia*" of Joachim Trithemius, who was an earlier contemporary of Abbot Thomas, seemed particularly promising; so I got that, and Selenius's "*Crypto-graphia*" and Bacon's "*de Augmentis Scientiarum*" and some more. But I could hit upon nothing. Then I tried the principle of "the most frequent letter", taking first Latin and then German as a basis. That didn't help, either; whether it ought to have done so, I am not clear. And then I came back to the window itself, and read over my notes, hoping almost against hope that the Abbot might himself have somewhere supplied the key I wanted. I could make nothing out of the colour or pattern of the robes. There were no landscape backgrounds with subsidiary objects; there was nothing in the canopies. The only resource possible seemed to be in the attitudes of the figures. "Job," I read: "scroll in left hand, forefinger of left hand extended upwards. John: holds inscribed book in left hand; with right hand blesses, with two fingers. Zechariah: scroll in left hand; right hand extended upwards, as Job, but with three fingers pointing up." In other words, I reflected, Job has *one* finger extended, John has *two*, Zechariah has *three*. May not there be a numeral key concealed in that? My dear Gregory,' said Mr Somerton, laying his hand on his friend's knee, 'that *was* the key. I didn't get it to fit at first, but after two or three trials I saw what was meant. After the first letter of the inscription you skip *one* letter, after the next you skip two, and after that skip three. Now look at the result I got. I've underlined the letters which form words:

DREVICIOPEDMOOMSMVIVLISLCAVIBASBATAOVT

RDIIEAMRLESIPVSPODSEEIRSETTAAESGIAVNNR
FTEEAILNQDPVAIVMTLEEATTOHIOONVMCAAT.
H.Q.E.

'Do you see it? "*Decem millia auri reposita sunt in puteo in at* . . ." (Ten thousand [pieces] of gold are laid up in a well in . . .), followed by an incomplete word beginning *at*. So far so good. I tried the same plan with the remaining letters; but it wouldn't work, and I fancied that perhaps the placing of dots after the three last letters might indicate some difference of procedure. Then I thought to myself, "Wasn't there some allusion to a well in the account of Abbot Thomas in that book the '*Sertum*'?" Yes, there was: he built a *puteus in atrio* (a well in the court). There, of course, was my word *atrio*. The next step was to copy out the remaining letters of the inscription, omitting those I had already used. That gave what you will see on this slip:

RVIIOPDOOSMVVISCAVBSBTAOTDIEAMLSIVSPDEE-
RSETA
EGIANRFEEALQDVAIMLEATTHOOVMCA.H.Q.E.

'Now, I knew what the three first letters I wanted were – namely, *rio* – to complete the word *atrio*; and, as you will see, these are all to be found in the first five letters. I was a little confused at first by the occurrence of two *i's*, but very soon I saw that every alternate letter must be taken in the remainder of the inscription. You can work it out for yourself; the result, continuing where the first "round" left off, is this:

"rio domus abbatialis de Steinfeld a me, Thoma, qui posui custodem super ea. Gare à qui la touche."

'So the whole secret was out:

"Ten thousand pieces of gold are laid up in the well in the court of the Abbot's house of Steinfeld by me, Thomas, who have set a guardian over them. *Gare à qui la touche.*"

'The last words, I ought to say, are a device which Abbot Thomas had adopted. I found it with his arms in another piece of glass at Lord D — 's, and he drafted it bodily into his cipher, though it doesn't quite fit in point of grammar.

'Well, what would any human being have been tempted to do, my dear Gregory, in my place? Could he have helped setting off, as I did, to Steinfeld, and tracing the secret literally to the fountain-head? I don't believe he could. Anyhow, I couldn't, and, as I needn't tell you, I found myself at Steinfeld as soon as the resources of civilization could put me there, and installed myself in the inn you saw. I must tell you that I was not altogether free from forebodings – on one hand of disappointment, on the other of danger. There was always the possibility that Abbot Thomas's well might have been wholly obliterated, or else that someone, ignorant of cryptograms, and guided only by luck, might have stumbled on the treasure before me. And then' – there was a very perceptible shaking of the voice here – 'I was not entirely easy, I need not mind confessing, as to the meaning of the words about the guardian of the treasure. But, if you don't mind, I'll say no more about that until – until it becomes necessary.

'At the first possible opportunity Brown and I began exploring the place. I had naturally represented myself as being interested in the remains of the abbey, and we could not avoid paying a visit to the church, impatient as I was to be elsewhere. Still, it did interest me to see the windows where the glass had been, and especially that at the east end of the south aisle. In the tracery lights of that I was startled to see some fragments and coats-of-arms remaining – Abbot Thomas's shield was there, and a small figure with a scroll inscribed "Oculos habent, et non videbunt" (They have eyes, and shall not see), which, I take it, was a hit of the Abbot at his Canons.

'But, of course, the principal object was to find the Abbot's house. There is no prescribed place for this, so far as I know, in the plan of a monastery; you can't predict of it, as you can of the chapter-house, that it will be on the eastern side of the cloister, or, as of the dormitory, that it will communicate with a transept of the church. I felt that if I asked many questions I might awaken lingering memories of the treasure, and I thought it best to try first to discover it for myself. It was not a very long or difficult search. That three-sided court south-east of the church, with deserted piles of building round it, and grass-grown pavement, which you saw this morning, was the place. And glad enough I was to see that it was put to no use, and was neither very far from our inn nor overlooked by any inhabited building; there were only orchards and paddocks on the slopes east of the church. I can tell you that fine stone glowed wonderfully in the rather watery yellow sunset that we had on the Tuesday afternoon.

'Next, what about the well? There was not much doubt about that, as you can testify. It is really a very remarkable thing. That curb is, I think, of Italian marble, and the carving I thought must be Italian also. There were reliefs, you will perhaps remember, of Eliezer and Rebekah, and of Jacob opening the well for Rachel, and similar subjects; but, by way of disarming suspicion, I suppose, the Abbot had carefully abstained from any of his cynical and allusive inscriptions.

'I examined the whole structure with the keenest interest, of course – a square well-head with an opening in one side; an arch over it, with a wheel for the rope to pass over, evidently in very good condition still, for it had been used within sixty years, or perhaps even later, though not quite recently. Then there was the question of depth and access to the interior. I suppose the depth was about sixty to seventy feet; and as to the other point, it really seemed as if the Abbot had wished to lead searchers up to the very door of his treasure-house, for, as you tested for yourself, there were big blocks of stone bonded into the masonry, and leading down in a regular staircase round and round the inside of the well.

'It seemed almost too good to be true. I wondered if there was a trap – if the stones were so contrived as to tip over when a weight was placed on them; but I tried a good many with my own weight and with my stick, and all seemed, and actually were, perfectly firm. Of course, I resolved that Brown and I would make an experiment that very night.

'I was well prepared. Knowing the sort of place I should have to explore, I had brought a sufficiency of good rope and bands of webbing to surround my body, and crossbars to hold to, as well as lanterns and candles and crowbars, all of which would go into a single carpet-bag and excite no suspicion. I satisfied myself that my rope would be long enough, and that the wheel for the bucket was in good working order, and then we went home to dinner.

'I had a little cautious conversation with the landlord, and made out that he would not be overmuch surprised if I went out for a stroll with my man about nine o'clock, to make (Heaven forgive me!) a sketch of the abbey by moonlight. I asked no questions about the well, and am not likely to do so now. I fancy I know as much about it as anyone in Steinfeld: at least' – with a strong shudder – 'I don't want to know any more.

'Now we come to the crisis, and, though I hate to think of it, I feel sure, Gregory, that it will be better for me in all ways to recall it just as it happened. We started, Brown and I, at about nine with our bag, and attracted no attention; for we managed to slip out at the hinder end of the inn-yard into an alley which brought us quite to the edge of the village. In five minutes we were at the well, and for some little time we sat on the edge of the well-head to make sure that no one was stirring or spying on us. All we heard was some horses cropping grass out of sight further down the eastern slope. We were perfectly unobserved, and had plenty of light from the gorgeous full moon to allow us to get the rope properly fitted over the wheel. Then I secured the band round my body beneath the arms. We attached the end of the rope very securely to a ring in the stonework. Brown took the lighted lantern and followed me; I had a crowbar. And so we began to descend cautiously, feeling every step before we set foot on it, and scanning the walls in search of any marked stone.

'Half aloud I counted the steps as we went down, and we got as far as the thirty-eighth before I noted anything at all irregular in the surface of the masonry. Even here there was no mark, and I began to feel very blank, and to wonder if the Abbot's cryptogram could possibly be an elaborate hoax. At the forty-ninth step the staircase ceased. It was with a very sinking heart that I began retracing my steps, and when I was back on the thirty-eighth – Brown, with the lantern, being a step or two above me – I scrutinized the little bit of irregularity in the stonework with all my might; but there was no vestige of a mark.

'Then it struck me that the texture of the surface looked just a little smoother than the rest, or, at least, in some way different. It might possibly be cement and not stone. I gave it a good blow with my iron bar. There was a decidedly hollow sound, though that might be the result of our being in a well. But there was more. A great flake of cement dropped on to my feet, and I saw marks on the stone underneath. I had tracked the Abbot down, my dear Gregory; even now I think of it with a certain pride. It took but a very few more taps to clear the whole of the cement away, and I saw a slab of stone about two feet square, upon which was engraven a cross. Disappointment again, but only for a moment. It was you, Brown, who reassured me by a casual remark. You said, if I remember right:

' "It's a funny cross; looks like a lot of eyes."

'I snatched the lantern out of your hand, and saw with inexpressible pleasure that the cross *was* composed of seven eyes, four in a vertical line, three horizontal. The last of the scrolls in the window was explained in the way I had anticipated. Here was my "stone with the seven eyes". So far the Abbot's data had been exact, and, as I thought of this, the anxiety about the "guardian" returned upon me with increased force. Still, I wasn't going to retreat now.

'Without giving myself time to think, I knocked away the cement all round the marked stone, and then gave it a prise on the right side with my crowbar. It moved at once, and I saw that it was but a thin light slab, such as I could easily lift out myself, and that it stopped the entrance to a cavity. I did lift it out unbroken, and set it on the step, for it might be very important to us to be able to replace it. Then I waited for several minutes on the step just above. I don't know why, but I think to see if any dreadful thing would rush out. Nothing happened. Next I lit a candle, and very cautiously I placed it inside the cavity, with some idea of seeing whether there were foul air, and of getting a glimpse of what was inside. There *was* some foulness of air which nearly extinguished the flame, but in no long time it burned quite steadily. The hole went some little way back, and also on the right and left of the entrance, and I could see some rounded light-coloured objects within which might be bags. There was no use in waiting. I faced the cavity, and looked in. There was nothing immediately in the front of the hole. I put my arm in and felt to the right, very gingerly . . .

'Just give me a glass of cognac, Brown. I'll go on in a moment, Gregory . . .

'Well, I felt to the right, and my fingers touched something curved, that felt – yes – more or less like leather; dampish it was, and evidently part of a heavy, full thing. There was nothing, I must say, to alarm one. I grew bolder, and putting both hands in as well as I could, I pulled it to me, and it came. It was heavy, but it moved more easily than I had expected. As I pulled it towards the entrance, my left elbow knocked over and extinguished the candle. I got the thing fairly in front of the mouth and began drawing it out. Just then Brown gave a sharp ejaculation and ran quickly up the steps with the lantern. He will tell you why in a moment. Startled as I was, I looked round after him, and saw him stand for a minute at the top and then walk away a few yards. Then I heard him call softly, "All right, sir," and went on pulling out the great bag, in complete darkness. It hung for an instant on the edge of the hole, then slipped forward on to my chest, and *put its arms round my neck.*

'My dear Gregory, I am telling you the exact truth. I believe I am now acquainted with the extremity of terror and repulsion which a man can endure without losing his mind. I can only just manage to tell you now the bare outline of the experience. I was conscious of a most horrible smell of mould, and of a cold kind of face pressed against my own, and moving slowly over it, and of several – I don't know how many – legs or arms or tentacles or something clinging to my body. I screamed out, Brown says, like a beast, and fell away backward from the step on which I stood, and the creature slipped downwards, I suppose, on to that same step. Providentially the band round me held firm. Brown did not lose his head, and was strong enough to pull me up to the top and get me over the edge quite promptly. How he managed it exactly I don't know, and I think he would find it hard to tell you. I believe he contrived to hide our implements in the deserted building near by, and with very great difficulty he got me back to the inn. I was in no state to make explanations, and Brown knows no German; but next morning I told the people some tale of having had a bad fall in the abbey ruins, which, I suppose, they believed. And now, before I go further, I should just like you to hear what Brown's experiences during those few minutes were. Tell the Rector, Brown, what you told me.'

'Well, sir,' said Brown, speaking low and nervously, 'it was just this way. Master was busy down in front of the 'ole, and I was 'olding the lantern and looking on, when I 'eard somethink drop in the water from the top, as I thought. So I looked up, and I see someone's 'ead lookin' over at us. I s'pose I must ha' said somethink, and I 'eld the light up and run up the steps, and my light shone right on the face. That was a bad un, sir, if ever I see one! A holdish man, and the face very much fell in, and larfin, as I thought. And I got up the steps as quick pretty nigh as I'm tellin' you, and when I was out on the ground there warn't a sign of any person. There 'adn't been the time for anyone to get away, let alone a hold chap, and I made sure he warn't crouching down by the well, nor nothink. Next thing I hear master cry out somethink 'orrible, and hall I see was him hanging out by the rope, and, as master says, 'owever I got him up I couldn't tell you.'

'You hear that, Gregory?' said Mr Somerton. 'Now, does any explanation of that incident strike you?'

'The whole thing is so ghastly and abnormal that I must own it puts me quite off my balance; but the thought did occur to me that possibly the – well, the person who set the trap might have come to see the success of his plan.'

'Just so, Gregory, just so. I can think of nothing else so – *likely*, I should say, if such a word had a place anywhere in my story. I think it must have been the Abbot. . . . Well, I haven't much more to tell you. I spent a miserable night, Brown sitting up with me. Next day I was no better; unable to get up; no doctor to be had; and, if one had been available, I doubt if he could have done much for me. I made Brown write off to you, and spent a second terrible night. And, Gregory, of this I am sure, and I think it affected me more than the first shock, for it lasted longer: there was someone or something on the watch outside my door the whole night. I almost fancy there were two. It wasn't only the faint noises I heard from time to time all through the dark hours, but there was the smell – the hideous smell of mould. Every rag I had had on me on that first evening I had stripped off and made Brown take it away. I believe he stuffed the things into the stove in his room; and yet the smell was there as intense as it had been in the well; and, what is more, it came from outside the door. But with the first glimmer of dawn it faded out, and the sounds ceased, too; and that convinced me that the thing or things were creatures of darkness, and could not stand the daylight; and so I was sure that if anyone could put back the stone, it or they would be powerless until someone else took it away again. I had to wait until you came to get that done. Of course, I couldn't send Brown to do it by himself, and still less could I tell anyone who belonged to the place.

'Well, there is my story; and, if you don't believe it, I can't help it. But I think you do.'

'Indeed,' said Mr Gregory, 'I can find no alternative. I *must* believe it! I saw the well and the stone myself, and had a glimpse, I thought, of the bags or something else in the hole. And, to be plain with you, Somerton, I believe my door was watched last night, too.'

'I dare say it was, Gregory; but, thank goodness, that is over. Have you, by the way, anything to tell about your visit to that dreadful place?'

'Very little,' was the answer. 'Brown and I managed easily enough to get the slab into its place, and he fixed it very firmly with the irons and wedges you had desired him to get, and we contrived to smear the surface with mud so that it looks just like the rest of the wall. One thing I did notice in the carving on the well-head, which I think must have escaped you. It was a horrid, grotesque shape — perhaps more like a toad than anything else, and there was a label by it inscribed with the two words, "Depositum custodi." '*

---

* 'Keep that which is committed to thee.'

www.ingramcontent.com/pod-product-compliance
Lightning Source LLC
Chambersburg PA
CBHW020659030726
47498CB00002B/568